Riding the Wind

a young adult novel

tracy wainwright

tlc

TLC Wainwright Publishing, LLC

VIRGINIA

Riding the Wind

Published by TLC Wainwright Publishing, LLC
P.O. Box 1001
Toano, VA 23168

Book design by Daniela Bergman, Dear Violet Boutique Photography
www.dearvioletboutique.com
First Printing: 2013

ISBN-10: 09899485-3-6
ISBN-13: 978-0-9899485-3-1

Tracy Wainwright

www.tracywainwright.com

This book is dedicated to Daniela, who was a great friend to me even when I was a crazy, young woman who didn't yet realize what it meant to be a child of God. I'm so glad you're now also my sister in Christ and have blessed me with your continued friendship and sharing your wonderful photography with me, for my covers and so much more.

To the Lord God Almighty, whom deserves all praise, I cannot believe You were willing to take a stubbornly independent, hard-headed young lady and gift her with Your Spirit and guidance to serve You in such unexpected ways. My prayer is that every word I write will bring glory and honor to Your name.

Tracy Wainwright

Chapter 1

Dana halted her climb up the stairs when a hand grasped her elbow. Her full cup of soda sloshed, barely missing her pant leg. She spun around. "Hey, what's the deal?"

Crystal leaned in and nodded to the arena. "Look."

She scanned the crowd milling below the stands.

"What–?" Dana gasped and narrowed her eyes. *She shouldn't be here.* "I can't believe she has the nerve."

Crystal shook her head. "I know. And with Stu Wells of all people. Look how she's hanging all over him."

Jeremy'd be devastated. She shaded her eyes with her free hand and squinted, examining the area past the arena to the holding pins and rider waiting area. "I don't see him."

Or Bo. She sighed and proceeded to her seat in front of Jeremy and Bo's parents.

Mrs. Singer waved a flashy hand at her. She never even paused her conversation with the petite brunette sitting beside her. What a contrast next to Mrs. Singer's thick build, bouncy bleach-blonde hair and boisterous personality.

Of course, Mr. Singer couldn't have been more dissimilar from his wife either. He nodded a hello to Dana and Crystal as they sat in the two empty spots, maintaining his silent vigil on the action in the arena. Poor Mrs. Singer. She didn't have anyone to talk to at home or in her job as a short-distance truck driver. No wonder she never closed her mouth while they were at the rodeo. Except when her boys rode, that was.

"So," Crystal leaned in whispering, "Do you think Stacy's here out of spite?"

"I don't know." Dana knew and liked Stacy. They'd spent lots of time together, dating brothers as close as Jeremy and Bo. She never would have described Stacy as vindictive. But she also never would have thought Stacy capable of–

"It's just plain cruel. Why can't she leave Jeremy alone?"

She had no answer. "Why's Stu here anyway? He doesn't ride or rope."

"His sister rides barrels, I think. But I've never seen him here before."

Dana shook her head. If only things had gone as planned. Then everyone would be oohing and aahing over Stacy's engagement ring by now. If only…

"Thank you, ropers," boomed the loudspeakers. "Everyone did a great job. Our next category of competition will ante up the action a bit. Our bull-riders have drawn and are ready. The competition's tight today, with several top rank riders and honkers. Our first competitor is strapped on and raring to go. Get the clock set boys, prepare the gate, and welcome Mason Collins."

Dana clasped her hands together and scanned the distant area again. She knew she'd find Bo amid the other anxious cowboys. A buzzer rang and out of the corner of her eye Dana saw the first bull leap out of the gate. She focused on the waiting riders, though. He'd be waiting for her. Searching for her. He always did. This was their moment.

Breaking into a grin, she locked eyes on him through the swarm of people. Bo's tall frame stood almost an inch over six feet. His sandy blond hair had mad highlights most girls would kill for. His black cowboy hat hid most of that beautiful hair now. She pictured the muscles she couldn't see as he stood behind the gates.

As Dana looked at Bo the rest of the world disappeared. She didn't move. He didn't move. For that moment, nothing else mattered. They were completely each other's. And that's all she needed to know. Then he broke their connection. His head turned and his jaw tightened.

Following his gaze, Dana groaned. Stacy & Stu. She jerked

her head back to watch Bo. He searched the area around him. Looking for Jeremy. Making sure Jeremy hadn't seen her.

He glanced her way once more before pulling the front of his hat down and striding towards the holding pins. His long legs swung over the gate behind pin number one as he spoke to the guys waiting there. He checked details she couldn't make out. When the buzzer sounded the end of the third ride, Bo climbed off the fence and mounted the waiting bull.

"A decent ride and a respectable score of seventy-eight for Corey McFallon."

Dana closed her eyes. She drew in the now-familiar smells of hay, manure, and leather, intermingled with fried food. *Bo, hang on and be careful.* She didn't give a hoot what score he earned. All she wanted was an uneventful ride.

An elbow in the ribs popped her eyes open. Crystal smirked. "Sending good vibes?"

"Of course."

"When's Bo up?"

The announcer blabbed on as she double-checked the pins. "After this one, best I can figure."

"Good figuring," a deep voice behind her said.

Dana jumped. She glanced back at Bo's dad. She'd almost forgotten he sat behind her. Not Mrs. Singer, who still regaled the poor lady on the other side of her with tales of wayward or newly-married-to-a-waitress truck driver stories. "Um, thanks."

Mr. Singer nodded.

Dana raised her eyebrows at Crystal. The eight seconds waiting for Bo's turn ticked by. But the same miniscule span of time would seem eternally longer during his ride.

The buzzer resounded and the rider hopped off, making a quick exit while the clowns distracted and corralled the bull to his escape route.

Dana leaned forward. The bull he'd drawn would make a big difference in the difficulty of the ride. And the score achieved. Based on too many discussions on the topic Bo and Jeremy wanted a tough animal to boost their score. She hoped for an easy one.

He tied his left hand down and squirmed to get situated.

"Next up we have Bo Singer, three year veteran and five time first place winner. He's drawn Cajun King, spicy like his name and thinks he's the boss. Let's see if Mr. Singer can hold on and temper this feisty aristocrat."

Great. Dana laced her fingers tightly around her cup.

A buzzer sounded. The gate swung open and Cajun King darted out. Bo's left hand stayed fastened in the rope as his body rocked and jerked. He matched each move the bull made.

Dana checked the clock. Five more seconds.

Bo's torso bounced side to side, frontwards, and back. He controlled every muscle. Every movement. Every action. He hung on with sheer will and determination. Another glimpse at the timer told Dana only two seconds remained.

Eight seconds. That's all he needed.

The buzzer reverberated. Dana clasped her chest with one hand as an attempt to calm her pounding heart. He'd made it. Still, though, he had to get off the bull and safely through the gate. Bo loosened his grip and skillfully leapt off and away from the erratic animal. The two clowns worked their magic to entice Cajun King away from Bo. He pumped his fist in the air, signaling he knew his score would be good.

Bo shuffled out of the arena and through the gates of safety. Dana held onto Crystal's arm as they waited on his score.

"And with that successful, skilled ride, Bo Singer takes the lead with a score of eighty-nine."

Dana burst into applause with the rest of the audience. Eighty-nine. He'd be hard-pressed to lose with a score that high. Her heart soared as she tried to catch another glimpse of him. He'd be stoked.

And in the best of moods for their date after. Her grin spread. It promised to be a good night.

~ * ~

Dana sipped the last of her soda as the announcer once again corralled the audience's attention.

"Next up, to battle his brother for first place is Jeremy Singer. A four year veteran, the older Singer has also taken first place five times. He's drawn Live Wire, a bull who's earned his name. If Singer can hang on, he'll give his brother some stiff competition for the lead."

Had Jeremy seen Stacy? Even if he had, maybe he'd still ride okay. She'd watched both him and Bo ride for months. Neither one of them had ever messed up. They always earned excellent scores and had a friendly competition going.

She smiled. Of course, she wanted Jeremy to score well, but hoped Bo stayed on top. The better the mood he was in, the better her night would go.

The gate swung open and the clock started its count. The bull lurched out of the gate sideways, slamming against it. Jeremy jerked to one side. His free hand worked frantically to unwrap his left hand. He couldn't get it loose. Live Wire flung Jeremy's body left and right and the crowd watched breathlessly.

Dana's mouth fell open as the bull tossed Jeremy, the boy she considered her adopted big brother, around like a piece of meat.

Chapter 2

Dana held her breath as the seconds, feeling like hours, ticked by. Jeremy struggled to untie his hand. Finally, he loosened the ropes enough to release his hand and attempted to leap off the bull. Instead of jumping off clear like he should have, he fell straight to the ground. The bull bucked twice before the waiting clowns coerced him away and out of the arena.

Jeremy lay still in the dirt. Dana exhaled when he turned his head to the side and groaned. As soon as the gate closed behind the bull, Bo raced in with a couple of the other bull-riders. The medical team arrived at Jeremy's side at the same time.

The medical technicians appeared to be questioning Jeremy while looking him over. He reached down towards his left leg and Dana squeezed Crystal's hand. It even seemed he might be talking to those close around him, although she couldn't be sure. He'd been hurt badly. The medical technicians hoisted him on a stretcher and carried him out of the arena. Bo stuck to his side.

Dana's heart swelled. Her man. He must be so worried. Her smirk dipped down as her eyebrows creased. He knew the dangers of bull-riding and had seen many friends get hurt. What was he going through watching his brother in so much pain?

The Singers moved past her row and raced down the bleachers. Those around them called out.

"It doesn't look that bad."

"He'll be okay."

"We're praying."

The Singers probably hadn't heard a word. Her own mind spun, slowing down her body's reaction. She shook off the daze, grabbed her purse, and began to descend the steps. There's no way she'd be left behind. Besides, Bo would need her.

Focused on the Singers, Dana raced down the bleachers and headed to the back area where she rarely ventured.

Oh, let him be okay.

She and Crystal rushed into the tent beside the always present ambulance. Two medics crouched over Jeremy. Mrs. Singer wrung her hands and wailed as she anxiously looked over the shoulder of one of the men.

Mr. Singer stood beside her, resting a hand on her back. Dana's gaze darted around and landed on Bo. He stood by Jeremy's head and gripped his hand. Jeremy lay with his eyes closed. His face was white and his lips were pulled tight. A soft moan escaped as he shifted his body weight.

How bad was he injured? She couldn't tell anything through the technician and Mrs. Singer. She looked back at Bo and took a step towards him. He met her gaze briefly when she reached for his free arm. Anxiety and…anger? She recognized the fire in his eyes. Jeremy must have seen Stacy. And Bo placed the blame for his accident squarely on her pretty blonde head.

Crystal tugged on her hand. She followed her friend's gaze to the fringes of the tent. Stacy Athens stood among a small crowd watching the drama. Stacy stood alone, no Stu in sight. She held her throat with one hand and wiped tears with the other.

Oh, Bo, don't see her.

He didn't. Yet. He clasped Jeremy's hand in his as the two medical technicians completed their initial examination. One looked not much older than Dana, maybe twenty. He had black hair, stood a foot taller than her, and was built like a football player. The other was shorter, maybe five-eight, with short, sandy hair. His slim frame capped off with a pair of overly thick glasses. He looked older, more like her parents age.

"How…is…he?" Mrs. Singer asked between sobs. "Is he…going to be…okay?"

"Ma'am," the older one said gently.

Mrs. Singer calmed and sniffled.

"The right leg was gashed by a screw on the gate. He's going to need stitches." He scrunched up his nose and paused. He sighed, as if he dreaded what he had to say next. "The left leg's the real problem. The bull's hoof came down on it after he fell." He hesitated again, pushed up his glasses, and sighed again.

"We won't know the extent of the damage until we get him to the hospital. But it doesn't look good."

Mrs. Singer fell against her much smaller husband and wailed. Mr. Singer flung his right foot back to brace himself as he wrapped his arms around her.

Tears flooded Dana's eyes. Would he be okay? The bull could have crushed his leg when its hoof came down. What if he couldn't walk again? Or ride. A shiver shot up her spine. Bo's arm flexed under her hand when she squeezed.

Jeremy groaned and turned his head away. Bo leaned over and whispered, "Don't you listen to them. You'll be fine."

Dana's heart accelerated. Bo was such a good guy. And a great brother. She loved those things about him. The all-to-familiar butterflies perked up and started flying around in her stomach. The fire of desire also ignited. It was crazy, but all she wanted to do at this moment was wrap her arms around his neck and dive into a thirty minute kiss.

How shallow. How could she stand there thinking about making out with Bo while his brother lay on a stretcher in excruciating pain?

The medical technicians moved Jeremy into the back of the ambulance and Bo pulled from her grasp as he turned to his mother. "I'll ride with him."

He stepped into the ambulance and locked eyes with Dana.

"Do-" The ambulance doors slammed shut. Dana dropped her shoulders. The flames of desire she'd felt moments before squelched like a bucket of dirt being thrown on a camp fire. Should she meet him at the hospital? Or wait for Bo to call her later?

Dana swatted a lone tear traveling down her cheek. Crystal squeezed her hand. She glanced at her friend, then eyed Bo's parents. Mrs. Singer's face crumpled and his turned stoic as the ambulance pulled away. Once it drove out of sight, Mr. Singer pushed his weepy wife towards the parking lot.

She had to go, too. She couldn't wait around wondering

what was happening.

Dana put her arm on Mrs. Singers'. "I'll meet you at the hospital."

"Oh, no, dear," Mr. Singer said. "You girls go on and enjoy yourselves. It's going to be a long night, there's no telling how long."

"Oh, I…" She floundered. She never knew how to talk to Bo's father. "Really. We want to be there. It doesn't matter if we're up late."

Mr. Singer looked at her as if she were five years old. "Bo will call you tomorrow, Dana. The family needs to be together right now."

Dana fought the urge to argue with the man, to yell that he had no right to keep her away from her boyfriend. She wanted to tell him off and show up at the hospital anyway.

But that wouldn't do her any good. Mr. Singer was Bo's dad. She'd be crazy to get on his bad side. From what Bo had told her, his dad could be awfully stubborn. She wouldn't take a chance on him keeping her from seeing Bo.

Fine. She wouldn't go where she wasn't wanted.

Dana turned on her heel and strode off to her car, Crystal following behind. She tossed her purse behind her, huffed into the driver's seat, and waited for the passenger door to close. She cranked the engine then cut it off.

"Dana?" Crystal asked. "Are you okay?"

She glared out of the windshield. "Fine."

Crystal waited. Dana glanced at her and rolled her eyes. "I'm fine."

Her best friend raised an eyebrow.

"Okay, I'm ticked. I can't believe his dad won't even let me come by and see how Jeremy is."

Crystal's eyebrow lifted a little more.

Dana let out a scream and laid her head on the steering wheel. "I know. It's a family thing. But how long have I been around, a part of the family? Jeremy's like my big brother. I'm worried."

"Dana…"

"Oh, all right. Whatever." She checked her watch. Only seven-thirty. Now what? She didn't want to go home. An empty house would be unbearable.

"What're you gonna do?"

"I don't know." She pressed her head against the steering wheel and rocked it back and forth.

"Max's having a party. Why don't we go?"

She didn't feel like going to a party, but didn't want to go home either. She longed to be with Bo, but that wasn't going to happen. "All right. Let's go."

~ * ~

Dana pulled into the field where a couple of dozen cars were parked. Crystal had talked the whole ride, trying to distract her. She was grateful for the company of her best friend. Otherwise, she'd go crazy.

These parties used to entice Dana. Everyone would be there. A cacophony of laughter, conversations, and drunken banter greeted her as she slammed the car door. She rolled her eyes. Did she really once call these people her friends? She considered getting back in the car, but one look at Crystal's hopeful face convinced her to stay.

Crystal'd had a crush on Max forever and he'd broken up with his girlfriend the week before. Besides, Dana didn't really have anywhere else to be. She bit her bottom lip.

She'd let Crystal have her chance. At least one of them will have a good time.

The night mirrored every other party Dana had gone to. The guys drank too much and acted stupid. The girls drank too much and threw themselves on the closest guy, the ones who weren't attached anyway. Everybody knew everybody and who was dating who and who was willing to hook up.

Dana spotted Max, surrounded by some of his football buddies. Crystal stopped short and caught her breath. *Guess she saw him, too.*

She shoved her hands into her back pockets. "I'll be okay. Go ahead."

"You sure?" Crystal arched an eyebrow.

"I'm sure." Dana gazed around the crowd. "I'll find *somebody* to talk to."

"You're the best friend ever." Crystal squeezed her in a hug and sprinted off.

She caught sight of Brooke and Kara on the other side of the fire. At least they wouldn't be too drunk, plus both played nice, not catty like most of the other girls. They were cheerleaders, like her. *Like I was.*

Cheerleading and dating a bull rider didn't go well together at Western Plain High School. She still could've tried out, but lost her desire.

"Dana." Kara waved. She waved back, forced a smile, and strolled over. Maybe they'd feel sorry for her.

"Brooke, Kara. What's up?"

Brooke flipped a lock of silky blonde hair back and took a sip from her cup. She looked flawless. Her jeans must've been a size four and the turquoise top she had on made her eyes look even bluer. If she weren't so nice, Dana would hate her.

"The usual."

"Yeah," Kara agreed. "I don't know why we even bother."

"Because there's nothing else to do." Brooke sipped from her cup again. She glanced around the field.

Kara studied Dana. "What are you doing here? You never come to these things anymore." She brushed back her short brunette hair with one hand, using the other to move the clip that was supposed to be keeping it out of her face. She always wore a clip, but her hair always slipped out and encroached on her face. There was a tiny scar by her hair line, probably the reason she only half attempted to keep it pulled back.

Kara was pretty. Not stunning like Brooke, but she got asked out plenty. She usually said no, but in a gentle, thoughtful way. Of course, that didn't stop the other girls from talking trash about her and the boys from calling her a tease behind her back. Dana knew the score. The girls were jealous and the guys were ticked Kara wouldn't go out with them. She had heard a rumor about her dating one of the football players before Dana had moved there, but not much else. Thinking about it, she couldn't remember one date Kara had been on since they'd met.

Kara gave Dana the, 'I asked you a question' look. The image of the ambulance door slamming shut brought tears to her eyes. "Jeremy got hurt."

Kara's eyes widened. "No!"

"What happened?"

"The bull slammed his leg against the gate as he was coming

out. That threw him off balance and he fell. The bull stomped on his other leg before the clowns got him away."

"Oh, how awful."

"Is he okay?"

Dana hooked her thumbs in her front belt loops. "I guess. They couldn't tell the extent of the damage to his leg. They took him to the E.R. for more tests. It looked ghastly, though."

"Oh." Kara leaned towards her. "That might mean no more riding."

"Not for a long time, anyway. Like I said, they didn't know anything for sure, but he'll probably be off his leg for a long time. It looked terrible."

"Poor Jeremy." Kara looked out into the darkness and readjusted the clip in her hair again. "He'll be crushed. And he's been through so much already."

Dana stared wide-eyed at her. What did she know? Surely she couldn't know about what broke Jeremy and Stacy up. Could she?

Kara had always shown interest in Jeremy. She was friendlier to him than other guys, but Jeremy had dated Stacy forever. An image of Kara and Jeremy talking by his car at the Tasty Freeze a couple weeks back flashed in her mind.

Dana coughed. "Yeah."

Kara and Jeremy? She formulated a casual way to ask Kara about the deal between her and Jeremy.

Brooke interrupted her thoughts. "I can't believe that happened. Jeremy's been riding forever. From what I hear, he's a perfectionist and is the bomb on the back of a bull."

"Well…." Dana hesitated. She hated to gossip. But was it really gossip? Stacy had shown up. But she didn't know for sure Stacy had anything to do with Jeremy's accident. Maybe he hadn't even seen her.

She shoved her hands in her back pockets. Brooke had a point. Jeremy had never messed up before. At least, not that she'd ever seen. It would have torn him up if he'd spotted Stacy. And how could he not? She'd traipsed all around the arena with Stu, as brash as a peacock.

"Well, what?" Brooke demanded.

Dana lowered her voice a notch. "Stacy was there."

Chapter 3

Kara puckered her lips and sucked in her cheeks, but remained stubbornly silent. Her eyes didn't leave Dana's face.

"What?" Brooke shrieked. "What in the world was Stacy doing there?"

"Shh." Dana looked around to make sure no one else was listening. "You don't have to tell the whole world. She was there with Stu Wells."

"Stu Wells? Are you kidding me? Why would he be at the rodeo?"

"His sister does barrels. I guess he wanted to watch her."

Kara narrowed her eyes. "You're being too kind, Dana. He couldn't give a flip about watching his sister ride a horse. He wanted to gloat and get under Jeremy's skin. That jerk tried to get Stacy away from Jeremy forever and wanted to flaunt that he finally got her. I bet he doesn't feel a bit sorry about the accident. He'll probably brag about it."

"He might get pummeled if he does," Dana hissed.

Brooke's eyes widened. "Why's that?"

"Bo's already livid Stacy had the nerve to show her face. If he thinks Stu brought her to spite Jeremy, he'll lose it. He already can't stand the sight of that girl. Let him get wind of this…"

"Well, who can blame him, after she-"

"Shh," Kara whispered. Her gaze led the other girls to a pair walking up to the trio.

Dana rolled her eyes. Jill and Amy. Two of the girls from the cheerleading squad, known to talk behind anyone's back and make life difficult for anyone who got in their way. They could smell gossip from a mile away. Normal people wouldn't barge into their hushed conversation. Clearly Jill and Amy weren't normal.

"What's up, chickadees?" Jill slurred.

Dana swallowed the desire to tell her off. Jill's main party plan revolved around getting drunk and hooking up with whoever volunteered for the job. Then, two days later, back at school and sobered up, she'd run her mouth about anyone and anything she thought would deflect attention from herself. Dana had caught wind of the spiteful things Jill said about her, especially since Dana quit the squad and began going out with Bo.

Dana crossed her arms and stared past her.

Brooke answered the invasive question. "We're just talking 'bout Jeremy Singer."

"Why in the world would you talk about *him*?" Amy looked at Dana and sneered.

"Grow up, Amy." Brooke rolled her eyes. "He had a bad accident tonight and is in the hospital."

"Really?" The edges on Amy's face softened some. "Is he okay?"

"Don't act like you care," Kara spit.

"Well, of course she cares." Jill took up for her friend. "We don't like anyone to get hurt."

Dana couldn't stand the hypocrisy a second longer. "Oh, please! A minute ago he wasn't worth talking about. All you care about is some juicy gossip to go spread."

Jill smirked. "Heartless, Dana. That's pure heartlessness. How are things with Bo?"

"Things are fine. He's with his brother." Disgusted, she turned to Brooke and Kara. "I'll check y'all later." She spun on her heel and headed across the field in search of Crystal. Time to go home.

Crystal was nowhere to be found. Dana paused on the outskirts of the group by the field where they'd parked and dug in her purse for her cell phone. She shot off a text, "Ready 2go. Where r u?"

She tapped her foot, waiting for the reply. None came. Slipping her phone open and closed several times without an answer, she snapped it closed one last time and tossed it back in her purse. Her eyes pierced the darkness, scanning for Crystal one more time. She wasn't by the bonfire. Nor by the pickup that had delivered and held the keg. Shadows from the fire played with her vision, convincing her she'd seen something only to have it vanish as quickly as a plate of hot wings set in front of a group of football players.

Dana squeezed her eyes shut. Maybe she should just go. Crystal was a big girl and could fend for herself.

Guilt pierced her heart. How could she leave Crystal not knowing what was going on? Crystal would never do that to her.

She looked towards her car, back across the field, then at her car again. "Come on, Crystal."

"Talking to yourself, Dana?"

She jumped and spun around. Chet Watkins. She stifled a groan. "Yeah, I didn't find anyone else around here worth talking to."

"Really?" He stepped closer. "Look no further. You're problems are solved."

Dana couldn't stop her eyes from rolling. "I never said I had a problem, Chet."

"Looks to me like your problem is being alone." He stepped even closer, breathing stale beer in her face. "We can take care of that. I know a little place where we can…talk."

She remained perfectly still and willed herself to stay in control. She stared at him. "You do know I have a boyfriend?"

He turned his head to one side, then the other. His gaze returned to meet hers. "Nope. I don't see anyone."

She leaned forward until her nose almost met his. "There's no doubt about it. You can't see anyone but yourself. Bo is my boyfriend whether he's here or not. You're a fool. And I'd rather talk to myself any day than talk to you."

Chet's mouth hung open as she stepped back, spun around, and stomped off to her car. She slipped into her seat with a huff and slammed her door. Could the night get any worse?

She grabbed her phone and texted Crystal again, "I'm leaving," then leaned her forehead against the steering wheel. What should she do? She couldn't leave Crystal. She couldn't stay here. Tears spilled down her cheeks.

She felt so alone, more than she had since…since moving to Texas. Since her parents had uprooted everything in her life and she had shut out the one she used to think she'd always depend on: God.

Was He still there and did He care about her at all anymore?

The image of herself at eight years old in a sleeveless, white dress on the day she was baptized flashed in her mind. That little girl believed in God and beamed for the photo with her parents after service that day.

Then those same parents had destroyed her life at fifteen by taking her away from everything she'd known. No amount of crying, screaming, bargaining, or praying had kept her in Northern Virginia. And the day they moved, she vowed she'd never depend on God again.

But sitting utterly, completely alone at that moment, with tears pouring down her cheeks, she craved for some kind of connection.

She wasn't sure she still believed the things she'd said back then. Or whether she should. Did it even matter?

The tears slowed as questions galloped around her head.

She swiped them away. God certainly hadn't answered her prayers when she'd begged Him to stay in Virginia.

A picture of Bo blasted to the front of her mind. Her mouth turned up in a weak grin. But, if she hadn't come to Texas, she wouldn't have met Bo.

Did God have anything to do with that? God hadn't been a part of her life in a long time and she saw no reason to ask Him for anything or consult Him on anything. Not until that moment.

She took a ragged breath and wiped her cheeks. She would try Crystal one more time. She fumbled in her purse for her phone. She jumped when someone knocked on the passenger side door.

Oh, let it not be Chet. I might lose it and run over his foot in my hurry to leave.

Crystal's face stared back at her through the window. She sighed with relief, hit the unlock button, and Crystal slid in the car.

"You okay?"

"Yeah." Maybe her friend wouldn't notice the tear streaks in the dark. "Where were you? I looked everywhere and texted you."

"With Max."

Dana heard the smile in her friend's voice. Crystal sounded a bit too happy. She flicked on the overhead light. "You didn't…"

Crystal's eye's grew round as barrels and she stuck her bottom lip out. "Of course not! What do you think I am?" Then she smiled. "We did kiss, though. And oh, I could have stayed there kissing him all night."

Dana grinned. At least Crystal had finally made progress with Max. "So, why didn't you?"

"I kept getting these pesky texts."

"But you didn't text me back."

"I did, check your phone. I told you I was coming."

"Oh. I didn't check it again. You're barely in time, though. I was 'bout to spin outta here."

"I know." Crystal's smile widened. "I needed an excuse to leave. If I'd stayed, I might have gotten myself in trouble."

"Glad I could help ya out. I'll have a life crisis any time for you."

Crystal laughed. "A life crisis. A little dramatic, don't you think. Jeremy's the one in the hospital, not you. Or Bo."

She chuckled. "Yeah. I guess he's having a little worse night than me."

She inhaled and then blew the air out through her taut lips. Her shoulders relaxed. She'd be okay. Tomorrow she'd get to see Bo and find out how Jeremy was. Everything would be fine.

She hoped.

Chapter 4

Dana rubbed her eyes and yawned before hitting the button to answer her phone. "Hello?"

"Hey, there."

Bo. Her mind raced. Something wasn't right. Something had happened. Then, like cold water splashing her face, it hit her. Jeremy. Stacy. The accident. Not going to the hospital. But he'd called.

"You there, babe?"

Dana cleared her throat. "Yeah, I'm here. Just takes me a minute to wake up."

"But I bet you're still gorgeous."

She smiled and sank back on her pillow. "Whatever. No need for flattery, you already have me."

"It's not flattery, darlin'. It's the God's-honest truth."

Dana squirmed, uncomfortable with the words she knew came from his heart. She glanced at the clock. A little after eight. "How's Jeremy?"

Bo inhaled sharply. "He's sleeping. I just got home. They took him into surgery around three and didn't get out until after six." He yawned.

She waited. Bo didn't like to be asked too many questions, but if she gave him enough room and time, he'd fill her in on the details.

"It's bad, Dana. His left leg is crushed. They pieced together the bone and pinned it all over. They sewed everything else back together, but there's no telling how everything will heal. Or if it'll heal. The doctor said worst case scenario, he'll never walk unaided again."

She gasped. "But, Bo. Surely…"

What? Jeremy had been so healthy and fit that he would bounce right back? Jeremy'd been through enough lately and didn't need this? No, none of those things changed the damage done to his body.

"What's the best case scenario?" she asked.

"What?"

She pulled the phone from her ear. His anger came across loud and clear. *He's not mad at you. Don't bite.* "You said 'worst case scenario'. What's the best?"

Bo harrumphed. "Best, I guess, is that he faces a couple more surgeries and six months of physical therapy and could possibly regain full use of his leg again."

She rolled over and propped her head on her free hand. "Okay. Well, we'll just work towards that."

"But there are no guarantees, Dana. My brother's laid up in a bed, broken and battered because that, that witch decided she hadn't hurt him enough."

She took a deep breath. "Bo, I know you think it's Stacy's fault, but –"

"But nothing. Jeremy never messes up. If she hadn't shown up and ruined his concentration, he could have ridden even that bull flawlessly. He might have even beaten my score." His voice lowered. "I wish he had beaten me."

She sighed. Bo had a point. Jeremy had an unblemished record. Even if he didn't stay on the full eight seconds, he'd always been ultra careful. Sloppy and careless didn't define his riding style. "Okay. You have a point. But being mad at Stacy isn't going to help Jeremy get better."

"No. Our family, the people who *really* love Jeremy, will help him get better. She just better stay out of my way."

"Bo, don't make it worse. Enough has happened. Let it go."

"It's not my style, Dana. You know that. I don't let go because something's difficult."

She rolled onto her back and closed her eyes. "I know."

The flowered clock her parents bought her when she was six ticked the seconds away.

Finally, Bo spoke again. "Listen, babe. I'm gonna go. I need a shower and some sleep. I'll call you later. K?"

"Of course. I love you."

Silence. She looked at the screen on her phone. A picture of her and Bo, instead of his name and number. He'd already hung up.

She tossed the phone on her bedside table and scooted down in her covers. Maybe she'd get some more sleep, too.

But sleep eluded her. The pictures of Jeremy's accident, Stacy's appearance, and her desperate need to escape the party last night swirled in her head.

Outside her bedroom, footsteps stole down the hall towards the kitchen. *Guess Mom and Dad are getting ready for church.*

Dana hadn't stepped foot in her parents' new church. She'd been too angry at God after they moved, and then she got used to sleeping in and padding around the quiet house on Sunday mornings. Who needed church, anyway? She'd done fine on her own.

Western Plain High had treated her okay overall. She could handle the gossip-mongers. Besides, they were at every school she'd ever attended. She'd fit in pretty well, had good friends, made good grades, and found Bo, whom she loved more than anything. Could God add anything to her life that she didn't already have?

A pocket of emptiness in her heart said yes, He could. But what, she didn't know.

She flung the covers off and got up. She peaked out her door and heard the coffee pot gurgling in the kitchen. The aroma of bacon drifted down the hallway. One of her mom's home-cooked breakfasts sure would be good. She hadn't had one in a long time. Not fresh, anyway. Her mom always made enough, probably hoping Dana would show up. Dana would find it in the microwave after they left, ready to be warmed.

Not today, though. Today, she'd have breakfast with her folks. And maybe, just maybe go to church with them, too.

~ * ~

"Dana," her mom exclaimed when she turned around from

the stove and faced Dana standing in the doorway. "What are you doing up?"

Her father lowered his newspaper, his raised eyebrows asking the same question.

"Can't a girl decide to have breakfast with her parents?" She strolled to the refrigerator, opened the door, and dug for the gallon of low fat milk.

"Yes, but…" her mom's voice trailed off.

Dana flung the door shut and reached in the cabinet for a glass. "But, what?"

"You're wearing a dress. I don't think I've seen you wear a dress in two years."

Heat flooded Dana's cheeks. She already felt silly. Maybe she should have stayed in bed. But no. She'd rather do almost anything than stay at home alone today. Even go to church.

"Yeah, well. I woke up and couldn't go back to sleep. I thought I might die of boredom if I hung out here all day by myself."

Her parents shot each other wide-eyed looks.

Her dad set the paper down in front of him and lifted his coffee cup to his lips. He sipped, then asked, "So, you're going to church with us?"

Dana took a swig of her milk. She leaned over her mom's shoulder and sniffed the pancakes bubbling in the pan. "Sure, why not? Those about ready?"

As if her play button had been pushed, her mom began flipping the pancakes. "Yes, just a minute longer. The bacon's on the table already."

"Great. Thanks." Dana pecked her mom on the cheek and slid over to the table. She set her half empty glass down and grabbed a piece of bacon.

Her dad eyed her as he sipped his coffee. "So, what's up?"

"Nothing. Like I said, I couldn't sleep."

Her mom set a plate of pancakes in front of her and she smothered them in syrup. Dana relished the first bite as her mom refilled her dad's coffee cup.

She was still chewing when he spoke again. "Come on, Dana. Surely there's more to it than that. You haven't gone to church with us for almost a year. And you complained about going for almost two years before that. What's up?"

She swallowed the bite, which now seemed like a big, fat ball of dough. She willed the threatening tears away. She'd made a mistake. Why did she ever think she could suddenly change her routine and not have questions asked? Her parents weren't overbearing or nosy. But they did notice things. Too much.

"Nothing's up." She pushed the dripping pancake pieces around with her fork, which moments before had been calling her name.

"Did something happen?" Her mom's soft voice asked from behind her.

"I, well…" She lost the battle and tears formed in her eyes. One slipped down her cheek.

Her mother slid into the chair next to her and put her hand on Dana's. "Something did happen. Did you and Bo have a fight?" The creases on her mom's forehead told her she suspected something much worse than a simple disagreement.

"No." She stared into the doughy, syrupy mess on her plate. "Bo and I are fine. Jeremy had an accident last night. Bo just got home from the hospital and called to update me."

"What happened?" Her mom sounded almost relieved.

"His leg got slammed into the gate as he came out of the chute and when he got himself free, he fell and the bull stomped on his other leg."

Her mom gasped and her hand flew to her mouth. Her dad, never shaken by anything, asked, "How bad was he hurt?"

She relayed the update Bo had given her moments before.

"Who's the surgeon?" Her dad, always the medical administrator.

"I don't know, Dad. Didn't think to ask that question." Why did she even try to talk to him?

"I'll call the hospital later and find out what I can."

She lifted her eyes. Had her dad really offered to help? "Thanks," she said, weakly.

The only reply he gave was taking a sip of his coffee and picking his paper back up.

"Mrs. Singer must be worried sick. I'll have to call her after church. Maybe I can take some dinner over there this afternoon."

Dana, appetite back, had to finish chewing before she replied. "Food doesn't fix everything, Mom."

"Well, of course not, dear, but it doesn't hurt. Besides I'm sure she's exhausted after a night in the hospital."

"I don't even know if she came home this morning. She could still be there."

"Well, I'll fix a casserole that can be frozen." Her mom popped up and headed towards the freezer to dig out whatever she had stored there.

She rolled her eyes. She'd never seen the Singers eat a casserole in her life. They were fried chicken and steak kind of people.

Bo loved steak. Maybe she should try to learn to grill sometime and fix him dinner.

Good grief. She sounded just like her mom. She didn't need to cook for him, she needed to be with him.

She glanced at the clock on the microwave. Almost nine. Her parents would be leaving soon. Did she still want to go? She certainly didn't want to have any more questions aimed her way, but the thought of being in the house by herself repulsed her. She'd end up watching the clock slowly creep until Bo called again. She gulped down the last of her milk as she considered.

"So, you'll be ready to go in ten minutes?" her mom asked, suddenly appearing at the table again.

"I don't know." She grabbed another slice of bacon.

"You really should come." Her dad folded his newspaper and stood. "We'll be in the car in ten." He downed the last swallow from his mug and walked out.

She tensed. How dare he tell her she should come? He needed to grow some manners.

"Honey," her mom broke into her thoughts, "it really would be nice. We've missed you on Sunday mornings.

Her mother always did calm the fires that raged between Dana and her dad. But was finding a way to get out of the house worth putting up with him and the phoniness of everyone and everything at church?

Chapter 5

Dana checked her phone. Bo still hadn't called. Or texted. But at least it was mid-afternoon now. Church and lunch with her parents and some friends helped the time to go by a bit faster.

She checked her phone again. Nothing. Not that she could miss it vibrating in her hand. But still. It was after two and he hadn't tried to reach her again. He couldn't be mad, could he? No. Not at her anyway. She shivered as his words resounded in her head.

'She just better stay out of my way.'

Bo had never been violent. Or mean, even. But she had gotten a few glimpses at his temper in the last couple of months. And it always seemed to be directed at Stacy. He wouldn't do anything about it though, she was sure.

Not as long as Stacy stayed away.

Her dad turned into their driveway and waited for the garage door to open.

Please, God. Just keep Stacy away.

Her phone buzzed, causing her to jump and her mom to turn around, questioning Dana with her eyes.

Bo's picture, name and number flashed on the screen. She let it vibrate two more times as the car came to a stop. Before her dad had cut off the engine and closed the garage door, she darted inside.

"Hello."

"Hey. You been running a marathon or something?"

Dana closed her bedroom door and flopped on her bed. "No. I was in the car with my folks."

"You? With the parental units? What gives?"

Dana flinched. She knew she'd face questions from her parents about going to church. She hadn't thought about Bo asking about it. He hated church. Said he wouldn't step foot in one unless it was his own funeral and he had no choice.

"We just got home from lunch."

"Lunch? I thought they did the church thing on Sundays."

"They do. We did. How's Jeremy?"

"What do you mean, 'we did'?"

"I mean I didn't feel like hanging out by myself all day and I went with them. It's no big deal. Now are you going to tell me about Jeremy or what?"

Silence. She fought the urge to scream and bit her bottom lip.

Whack. Had he just thrown something?

She waited.

"Not much has changed. He's doped up on pain meds and they're running more tests today. My grandmother's at the hospital and my folks should be home soon. I'm going to head out after supper and stay with him tonight."

Dana released her lip and it fell beyond its normal spot to a pout. "So I won't see you?"

"I don't know. Want to come over now?"

"My mom wants me to wait for her. She's making a casserole to bring over. I think she wanted me to drive her over. I don't know how long it'll take."

"Okay, so that's my fault?"

Tears brimmed in Dana's eyes. Everything was going wrong. "No. Of course not. Maybe I can get her to bring it early. What time are you leaving?"

"I don't know exactly, Dana. Seven or eight. Things aren't exactly normal around here."

She swallowed down the lump in her throat. He's not mad at me. He's tired and worried. "Okay, that's plenty of time. We'll be there by five. I promise."

"Fine."

"Bo?"

"What, Dana?"

"I love you."

He sighed. "I love you, too. I'm sorry, Dana. I don't mean to bite your head off. I'm just–"

"I get it. But I still have feelings."

"I know and I am sorry. I do love you. And I do look forward to wrapping my arms around you and covering those pouty lips with mine."

She rolled onto her back and grinned. "Yeah. That'd be nice."

She hung up and hugged the phone to her chest. He did infuriate her, but he also sent her mind and body crazy with that deep, twangy voice of his.

She jumped off her bed and threw her phone on her dresser. Now to get her mom moving on that casserole.

~ * ~

The last shred of doubt melted away as Dana stood with Bo's arms wrapped around her. A twinge of guilt at the pure joy she felt tugged at her as she pictured Jeremy lying in the hospital. She opened her eyes and gazed across the field in front of her. A group of cows grazed a few hundred yards away. On the opposite side of a white picket fence, a couple of horses played, nosing each other, braying and pawing the ground.

A gentle breeze lifted Dana's hair and whipped it around. She drew it to the side, holding it in a mock ponytail with one hand. She grinned at Bo. "Sorry."

He leaned down and kissed her, then straightened and pulled his black cowboy hat back down into position. "It's fine. I love your hair." He wrapped his hand around it, pulled her head back, and kissed her again.

Pulling away breathless, she turned back to face the fields and leaned against him. Being a city girl, born and raised, she never would have thought country living would feel so right. But there, in Bo's arms, watching acres of nothing but a few animals roaming around, she relaxed and felt at home.

"So, how do you think the moms are doing?" Bo broke into her reverie.

She chuckled. "Who knows? Either your mom's shocking mine with her latest truck driving story or mine's boring yours to death with her latest recipes."

Bo laughed the deep, hearty laugh Dana loved. "If your mom does that, mine just might fall asleep standing up."

Dana cackled at the picture of Bo's mom, built like a football player, slowly tipping over and landing with the crash of a hundred year tree being felled to the ground. "I could picture my mom's face," she shook with laughter, "standing by your mom, fallen to the floor asleep. She'd either start praying over her or cook something else."

Bo's laughter trailed off and his body tensed.

Oh, she'd done it again.

"Well, you can tell her to save her prayers. They don't do any good."

"Maybe. Maybe not."

"They don't." His voice came hard and cold.

She hesitated, then plunged ahead. "I put Jeremy on the prayer list this morning."

He spun her to look at him. His jaw tight, he spoke through his clenched teeth. "Why would you do that, Dana? Why do you have to go share my personal business with people I don't know?"

She considered backing down. Apologizing. But no. She hadn't done anything wrong. Her spirit told her that. "They weren't strangers. They're mostly kids at school. And they were different." She stared out across the fields. That morning at church had been as different from her old church as country life was from the busy city life of Northern Virginia she'd grown up in. She looked at him squarely.

"It wasn't the kids that lie and gossip. Well, most of them weren't." She shook her head. "Anyway. Some of them had already heard and seemed genuinely concerned. They wanted to pray for him." She lowered her eyes and her voice. "Pray for y'all."

"They can keep their prayers." He plucked a blade of grass off the ground and stuck one end of it in his mouth, playing with it. "And what do you mean, for us?"

She averted her eyes once again. "I mean they wanted to pray for your whole family. That you'd be comforted while Jeremy's in the hospital." And that you'd come to know Jesus. But she couldn't say that. She hadn't exactly been living a life of witness for

Jesus. And besides, it might send Bo over the edge.

"The only comfort I'll get is when Stacy pays for what she did. If she hadn't shown up strutting her stuff, my brother would be in the barn cleaning or fixing something right now. Not laid up in the hospital."

Dana bit her bottom lip. There was no use in arguing with him. The fire in his eyes and set jaw told her she wouldn't get anywhere. *Lord, help Bo forgive. And help him see You.*

She felt rusty at prayer, but her body relaxed. She stepped close to him and wrapped her arms around his waist. "Hey."

The only muscle he moved was the one twisting the grass blade in his mouth.

"Hey," she repeated.

He looked at her.

She reached up and kissed his neck, right below his left ear. The spot he loved her to kiss. Then she met his gaze. "It'll be okay. It's not now, but it will be. Don't let Stacy ruin us, too."

Bo glared at her. Then, slowly, his face softened. "I don't know if everything will be okay. Not until Jeremy's better. But you're right. I won't let that witch get between us." He wrapped his arms around her.

Dana laid her head on his chest. "No. It's best not to think of Stacy at all."

Chapter 6

Dana slammed her locker and leaned against it. She glanced over Bo's shoulder at the clock hanging from the ceiling. Three minutes left.

"I'm glad you're here today. Two days at school without you were unbearable."

He cocked his head and gave her a lopsided grin. "Yeah. Well, sitting in the hospital hours on end was like a vacation."

She didn't know if he was kidding or not. He didn't care for school, but she couldn't imagine it'd been pleasant to spend the last few nights in the hospital. Of course, he wasn't the one laid up and on constant pain meds.

She reached for his hand. "Maybe I can go with you after school."

Instead of giving her an answer, his eyes darted to the left and he groaned.

"What?" She looked the same direction and recognized Katherine Veneris from the Sunday school class she'd visited.

Bo rolled his eyes. "I haven't even made it to my first class and this is the third one."

"The third what?"

Katherine stopped in front of them. "Hey, Dana. Hey, Bo. How's Jeremy? I was so sorry to hear about his accident. We've been praying for him. I know he'll be good as new in no time."

Bo pressed his lips together, his expression blank.

"Well, I'd better get to class. See you around."

"No," Bo said after Katherine waltzed off.

Dana stared at him. "No, what?"

"I don't think you should come to the hospital this afternoon." His jaw twitched. "But we do need to talk. I'll call you when I get home."

Her mouth fell open. Before she had a chance to reply, Bo sauntered off down the hall. Tears filled her eyes as she trudged off in the opposite direction to her first class.

Now what? He doesn't want me with him at the hospital.

His words boomeranged around her mind. 'We need to talk.'

She slid into her seat as the tardy bell rang. Her economics teacher began to drone on about the gross national product and supply and demand.

What did he want to talk about? They were good. He'd said so just a couple days before. He couldn't want to break up. She hadn't done anything that was wrong.

"…paper will be due a week from Friday…"

Dana opened her notebook and scribbled the details of the massive research project being laid out in front of her.

Great. Ten days to research the economic system of some third world country while her life fell apart.

She laid her forehead on her notebook as her teacher moved on to the current day's most-boring-lecture-ever contest entry.

God, help me. Help me keep Bo. Help me know what to do.

~ * ~

Dana clicked save on her laptop and answered her phone. Her heart thudded like the hoofs of a horse racing around barrels.

"Hey."

"Hey."

"How's Jeremy?"

"Better. Today was a better day."

"Good." She pushed her chair back, curled her legs underneath her, and held her breath.

He broke the silence. "Listen, I'm sorry about this morning, but I can't stand all the wimpy, trust-in-God, I'm-praying-for-you stuff. It's driving me crazy."

Dana blew out the breath she'd been holding. Okay, so maybe it wasn't her. "I know you're worried about Jeremy and you're angry, but why's this such a big deal? I mean, I'm not exactly gung-ho on the God thing, but these people are sincere. And it doesn't hurt."

"It does hurt."

Her mind spun. She had been mad at God. She'd shut Him out of her life. But she'd never viewed praying or talking about God as bad. She shook her head. "I don't get it, Bo."

"Dana, you've met most of my family."

"Yeah. Okay…"

"Have you ever noticed that you've never heard anything about my dad's father?"

She thought back to every family event she'd gone to. To conversations around the large oak table in the Singer's kitchen. Aunts, uncles, cousins, Mrs. Singer's parents who lived on the adjacent farm. She'd met Bo's Grandma Singer once. But never had she heard one whisper, one tidbit, about his Grandpa Singer. "I never thought about it, but no."

"My grandfather was a preacher. Every Sunday he would holler about how sinful everyone was and how they needed to turn to God, that we should be grateful He didn't come down and wipe us all out. Then, he'd go to work at the factory all the other days of the week, come home, drink himself into oblivion, and try to beat sin out of my dad."

Dana's hand flew to her open mouth. A horse whinnied in the background.

"I…don't…need…that…kind…of…God." Bo almost sounded out of breath.

What he said didn't match up with anything she'd been taught about God. "But…but that's not God, Bo. That was your grandfather. He got it all wrong." Verses about God's love memorized as a child swirled in her head. The love her parents, well, her mom, had always shown her. Her dad had always been distant, but never cruel. Never violent.

"Dana, understand me. My dad was beat almost every day of his childhood by a man who supposedly studied the Bible and knew God. I want nothing to do with it."

She uncurled her legs and stood. She paced the small space between her bed and desk. Her mind spun.

God loves you. He sent His Son for you. He has a good plan for you.

"But Bo, if you could just get to know the things I've been taught. Know the love of God."

"Read your own Bible, Dana. It's not all daisies and butterflies. It's also stoning, and wrath, and anger, and God striking people dead." Bo lowered his voice a notch. "And quit trying to preach at me and acting like you believe in all that garbage. I don't understand why when I need you to be there for me, to just be my girlfriend, you have to go and get all churchy on me."

"I didn't…" her voice trailed off. The truth was she had. When she'd met Bo and they'd began dating, God had been absent from her life. Kicked out, really. She'd booted Him like last year's prom dress.

So why was she so staunchly defending Him now? She'd allowed the topic of God to creep into almost every conversation she'd had with Bo since the accident. What in the world was happening to her?

"Bo, I'm sorry. I didn't know about your dad and I really didn't mean anything by it." She plopped onto her bed.

"I know you didn't. But understand, I want nothing to do with God, nothing to do with prayer, and don't want to hear anything about it from you again."

Chapter 7

Burning embers took fire in her belly, consuming and overpowering Dana's confusion about Bo's passion and pity for his father. He had no right to tell her what to do.

Biting her bottom lip and squeezing her eyes shut, she took several deep breaths before responding. She didn't want to fight with Bo. She wanted to wrap her arms around him. And if not bringing up God would allow her to do that, then so be it. She didn't understand it all herself.

"Okay, Bo. I get it. No big deal. Now, tell me about Jeremy. Have the doctors said when he might come home?"

He sighed. "A few weeks. Two, maybe three. Then he'll have therapy. But at least he'll be at home."

"Yeah, that'll be good."

"Hoo boy, it will."

"So, maybe I can come see him one day. You know, he is my only big brother."

She could see the grin she knew had crept on Bo's face. He loved that she'd adopted his brother.

"Yeah. It couldn't hurt. I wanted to be alone today, but as it turns out, that wasn't the case."

Dana raised her eyebrows. "Yeah?"

"Yeah," Bo's voice, now relaxed, sounded teasing. "Kara

came by."

Dana's eyes grew as round as barrels. "What?"

He chuckled. "I know. I asked Jeremy about it after she left and he said they're friends. They've been talking for a few weeks, but it's nothing more."

She rolled onto her back. "I'm not so sure. You should have seen her face when I told her about the accident."

"I'm not so sure either." He paused, then asked, "Hey, when did you tell her? My mom said she'd called on Sunday to check on him."

"Saturday night." She immediately regretted her words.

"Saturday night. Where?"

"At Max's party." She bit her lip, waiting.

"You went to a party after Jeremy's accident?" He hated those parties and didn't like her going alone, but his voice didn't hold the anger she'd expected.

"Crystal insisted. I couldn't be with you and she wanted to take advantage of Max's newfound unattached status. It was no big deal. We didn't stay long anyway."

"And?"

"And, what? Kara and Brooke were there. Some of the other cheerleaders were there. They didn't make good company and I left."

"That's it?"

She hesitated. She'd purposefully left out mentioning her chat with Chet. He stood only a ladder rung above Stacy on the list of people Bo couldn't stand. He'd never told her why, but always said he'd rather scrape horse manure off ten sets of horse shoes than spend five minutes with Chet. But, if she didn't say something and someone had seen them talking, even if it was more him drooling and her telling him off, Bo would almost for sure find out.

"Chet was there," she mumbled.

"Of course he was. And?"

"And obnoxiousness oozed from his every pore and I told him to get lost. End of story."

"So, do I need to go remind him who you belong to?"

Dana knew she shouldn't enjoy it, but it made her tingle from head to toe when Bo got jealous and declared she was his. She grinned. "No. I made it clear."

"Good. Because you are mine."

A new wave of tingles shot down her body. "And I like it that way."

"Me, too."

"You think you could get to school a little early tomorrow? I'll bring some biscuits and coffee and we can have breakfast in my car."

"How about dessert?"

She giggled. "My mom never lets me have sweets before lunch. 'A fruit or vegetable first,' she always says."

"I'll bring some orange juice." His voice turned husky. "That counts as a fruit, right?"

She squeezed her eyes shut. The tingles all met in her stomach, igniting fireworks more potent than the ones at the Houston rodeo. Then, like a sprinkler system clicking on to douse the fire, the words 'be holy because I am holy' pushed their way to the forefront of her mind. Her thoughts certainly weren't holy. They hadn't been in a long time.

"You can bring orange juice, but we're just going to eat breakfast, okay?"

"Okay … everything all right?"

She forced her cheerful voice. "Everything's fine. It's just… you drive me crazy and we're going to be in the school parking lot and all."

Bo chuckled. "You do have a point. Okay, just breakfast. I'll see you at quarter to seven."

Dana hung up and stared at the ceiling. What was wrong with her? If only things could go back to the way they were just a few days before.

~ * ~

"Hey, Dana."

She turned to see Katherine rushing down the hall, darting past the multitudes of students slamming their lockers and heading towards the exits.

"Hey, Katherine."

"I forgot to tell you earlier this week. Our Sunday school class is doing a scavenger hunt tomorrow. It'd be great if you could come."

She pursed her lips, then answered. "Sounds fun, but Bo's

riding tomorrow. I don't miss his rides."

Katherine's jaw dropped. She stared at Dana as if she'd sprouted horns on her head. "He's riding again?"

Dana had asked herself the same question. She'd asked Bo the same question. 'It's what Jeremy wants,' he'd said. Dana swallowed the lump that rose when the pictures of Jeremy lying on the arena ground came to mind. "He is."

"How…" She blinked several times. "How could he even think of getting on a bull again? Jeremy could've been killed. He may never walk again."

Dana hugged her books to her chest. Maybe it would relieve the tightness in her chest. "It's what he loves. Jeremy wants him to get back out there. To represent both of them." The tightness increased. "He insists."

"But can't you talk him out of it? Doesn't he understand how dangerous it is?"

An ironic cackle escaped Dana's throat. "Oh, he understands. All too well. That's part of the draw."

Katherine stared at her, shifting from one foot to the other. She opened her mouth then closed it again.

The corners of Dana's lips turned up. "I know. It makes no sense. But it's who he is. To take him off the bull would be like cutting his leg off, not just having it crushed."

Katherine shook her head. "I don't get it."

Her smile widened. "I don't either, but I love him. That means every Saturday night he rides is a Saturday night I'll be at the rodeo."

Katherine sighed. "Well, I guess I understand. We'll miss you, though." Her face brightened. "But we'll see you Sunday, right? You'll be back at church?"

"I … I'm not sure. I haven't really thought that far." She hadn't talked to Bo about what he planned to do Sunday. But she'd had such a sense of peace the week before. A calm and comfort she hadn't felt in years.

"Oh, I hope so. It was great having you last week." Katherine glanced around her at the almost empty hallway. "Well, I guess I'd better get going. I'm supposed to be at work in a few. See ya." She spun on her heel and sprinted away.

Dana glanced at the hanging clock. Bo was probably fuming by now. She texted him, "I'm coming."

She dashed towards the exit, pushed the door open, and stopped short of running into the figure standing on the other side.

She looked up and rolled her eyes.

"Hey, gorgeous," Chet drawled.

"Good-bye, Chet." She stepped around him.

His footsteps fell in line with hers. "Aww. Come on. Don't be like that."

"Take a hint. I'm taken and not interested."

"Surely one of these days you'll come to your senses and drop that cowboy. I'll be waiting so you can know what it's like to be with a real man."

She stopped and glared at him. He stood next to her with a stupid grin pasted on his face. She narrowed her eyes.

He raised his hands. "Okay, okay. But I'll be here whenever you change your mind." He laughed. "Or maybe I won't. And then you'll be sorry."

She blew at a strand of hair and headed towards her car. Great. Bo had beaten her there and saw the whole thing.

Chapter 8

Bo wrapped his arm around Dana and drew her close. "Hey, there."

His lips covered hers, drowning out her reply. She pulled away, looking at him with wide eyes, breathless.

"Guess I should be grateful to have a girlfriend to be jealous of."

She followed his line of vision. Chet stood by his car across the parking lot talking to another football player, his gaze aimed their way.

She giggled. "You're showing off."

"Yeah, well. You're mine to flaunt."

She leaned up and melted against his muscular chest as they kissed again. She laid her head on his shoulder and sighed. She'd love to have that single moment last forever.

"All right. We better get going."

"Yeah. I'm actually looking forward to seeing Jeremy. I can't believe I haven't seen my big brother since the accident. A week is entirely too long."

"It's best that you waited." Bo shivered. "He looks a lot better and isn't so doped up on drugs."

She looked up at him. "Is it true they might let him come home next week?"

Bo's face lit up. "If things keep going well, definitely."

"Well, we'll just…" She almost said, 'pray for that.'

"We'll just what?"

Dana rubbed her sweaty palms on her jeans. "Hope he keeps getting better. Now, let's get going. I want to see my big brother."

~ * ~

Dana squeezed Bo's hand and smiled at Jeremy. "Welcome home!" she sang with the rest of his family.

His grin shone bright as he wheeled out of the family van into the front yard.

Bo released her hand and sauntered over to the spot where Jeremy'd stopped his wheelchair. He grasped his brother's arm. "Good to have you home, Bro, but you're not going to be much help in that contraption."

Jeremy winked at Dana. "Well, it's about time you pulled your weight around here. I figure you've got a year or two of catching up to do."

"It better not take you that long to get back on your feet or I'll be building a ramp in the barn so you can at least brush a horse."

Jeremy's laugh rang like music in her ears. The few times she'd visited him in the hospital he'd barely cracked a smile. Being home had begun to heal him already.

She slid her hands into her back pockets as she watched the family usher him inside. She stared at the door after the last person went in. A breeze swept a lock of golden hair in her face and she looked up into the crisp, clear blue sky. She tucked it behind her ear.

I belong here. She closed her eyes and inhaled the smell of hay, horses, and manure. A year ago she'd have been repulsed. Now she could envision herself living there. With Bo. He'd already talked about his plans to build a house on the back of his parents' property. *Our home. One day.*

"Whatcha doin'?"

Dana jumped and opened her eyes to look straight into Bo's.

He grinned. "Do I make you nervous?"

"No. Just lost in thoughts."

He wrapped the fingers of his hand around hers. "Thoughts about me?"

"Yes."

"And?"

"And nothing." She rose onto her toes and kissed him. "Let's go inside. Join the party." She pulled him by the hand and walked towards the house. She stopped short, as he held tight to her hand and kept his feet planted in their place.

"So were they good thoughts?"

Heat flushed her cheeks. "Yes. Always. Now let's go."

"Maybe we'll take a walk to the barn and visit the horses. Talk a little about those thoughts." His eyes gleamed.

She reached up and brushed his lips with hers. Oh, how she loved those lips. He kissed the tips of her fingers. She gazed into his eyes. "I –"

"Bo. Dana. Y'all coming in or what? We're cutting the cake."

She turned to face Bo's cousin Natasha and smiled. The twelve-year-old practically became Dana's shadow whenever the family got together. "Sure, Natasha. We're coming."

Once again Bo pulled against her as she stepped towards the house.

"Bo, stop it. We really have to go. It'll be noticed for sure if we don't go in now."

The twinkle in his eyes reached to the corners of his mouth. "Oh, I'm going in. But if I want cake, I've gotta beat you." He dropped her hand and dashed towards the front porch steps.

She chased after him, catching up as he stopped to open the door. "Sorry, no cake for you." She laughed and squeezed past him through the tiny space he'd created.

~ * ~

The homemade ice cream melted in Dana's mouth. Another country treat she'd never been exposed to in the suburbs of Northern Virginia.

"So, you ready to do some real work yet? A week home is long enough of a break."

Jeremy shoveled a huge spoonful of peach ice cream into

his mouth. "This is all the shoveling I'm going to be doing for a while, little brother. You're still in charge of the manure."

"All right. I'll give you a few more days. But I'll be talking to that physical therapist of yours. She needs to push you a little harder."

Jeremy took another bite and mumbled, "Yuff rife."

"I'm telling you. She's not working you enough. She-" Bo narrowed his eyes. His jaw twitched.

Dana reached across the table. "Bo?"

He didn't move a muscle. She turned to follow his gaze outside the window, but didn't see anything. She jumped when he stood and shoved his chair back so hard it crashed onto the floor. She looked at Jeremy and he shrugged his shoulders. The front door slammed shut.

"Don't. Don't even bother getting out of your car."

A car door thumped. She hopped up and followed Bo outside. Her heart paused a couple beats. Stacy's slim figure stood next to her canary yellow Mustang parked in the grass next to Dana's car. Bo towered over her and glared at her, fists clenched by his sides.

"You have no right to be here. Jeremy doesn't want to see you."

"Why don't you let him speak for himself? I just want to see if he's okay."

"As if you cared. You're the reason he's hurt."

Stacy's hands flew to her hips. "*I'm* the reason? Oh, get over yourself, Bo. It was a sloppy ride on a bull. What'd I do, hypnotize the beast to throw him off and stomp on him?"

Bo took a step towards Stacy and Dana rushed down the stairs to his side. She grabbed his arm.

"Listen. You are not wanted here and you'd better watch what you say."

"Oh, yeah? Or what?"

Bo's muscles flexed under Dana's palm.

"Or–"

"Bo."

His arm relaxed and he turned towards the house. Jeremy sat in the open doorway. His shoulders slumped and his head leaned to one side.

"It's okay, Bo. Let her come in."

"You don't have to do that, Jeremy. You don't have to put up with her anymore."

"It's okay. Really."

Dana looked from Jeremy to Bo as they spoke in silent brother language. Bo stepped aside, clearing the path to the front porch.

Stacy brushed past. "Thanks," she muttered.

Bo moved towards the barn as soon as the door shut. Dana followed.

"Not now, Dana."

"Bo, I just wanna be with you." Calm you down. Distract you. Something.

"I'd rather be alone." He shrugged her hand off his arm and charged across the grass.

"Let it go, Bo. Jeremy's a big boy. He can take care of himself."

Bo stopped and pivoted. "Let it go? She broke his heart, stomped on it, killed … almost killed him. No, I won't let it go. I don't want her in my house."

"It's his house, too. I'm sure he knows what he's doing."

His eyes narrowed. "I'm sure he's not at his best right now. And I said I want to be alone."

He spun around and headed off.

Chapter 9

Tears sprung to Dana's eyes. Why did she always get the brunt of his anger when it came to Stacy? Every time things seemed to be perfect, something came along and messed it up.

It's not about me. It's just that I'm here. She watched him go around the corner of the barn and lifted her eyes upwards. *God, I know I've been coming to you a lot lately. Please help Bo forgive Stacy. I hate seeing him so angry.*

She turned back to the house and crept up the stairs and through the front door. Stacy's voice filtered in from the den.

"I'm sorry, Jeremy. Can't you get that through your thick skull? It's the worst mistake I've ever made."

Dana quietly closed the door behind her and stayed in the entryway.

"You're right. It was the worst mistake you've ever made. And I'm sure you're sorry. But that doesn't change the facts. You have to live with what you did. I don't have to have you in my life."

"I still love you, Jeremy." Crying broke up Stacy's words. "I never wanted to lose you. That wasn't part of the plan."

"None of it was part of the plan, Stacy. You were to finish high school, get your beautician's license and then we could get married. But it got screwed up. We both screwed up. And you ended it."

Stacy's sobs filled the air. She sucked in a deep breath. "I did it for us. Why don't you understand that? How could we do anything if we had a baby right now?"

"It wouldn't be easy. But the baby was already here. It was ours. Mine. You never took that into consideration."

"I know." She hiccupped. "And I'm sorry. I can't change it now. I'd take it back if I could, but I can't."

"And I can't take you back. I don't love you anymore."

Stacy's sobs ricocheted through the otherwise silent house. A door slammed shut, shaking the whole house. Dana tiptoed to the edge of the wall and peeked around it. Stacy sat alone on the sofa, face in her hands, tears pouring onto her lap. She was a stupid, selfish girl, but her heartache tugged at Dana.

She took a deep breath and walked over. She sat down and put her arms around Stacy, holding her as she cried.

Stacy hiccupped a few times and with a shuddering sob, the tears slowed. She raised her eyes to Dana. "I'm…a…mess."

She grinned. "Yeah. You are."

"Thanks for … not being mean."

Dana grabbed a handful of tissues from the coffee table and. Stacy dabbed her cheeks and eyes.

"I know Bo hates me. I think Jeremy doesn't care anymore."

"He cares. But he's hurt. Badly."

Stacy's shoulders shook and she let out a sigh. "I know. I really am sorry."

"I'm sure you are. But he needs his space. Especially now."

Stacy hung her head. "I had to see him. To see if he was really okay. I guess he is. And he isn't."

"He will be okay."

"Will I ever be?"

Stacy's question stirred a quiet place in Dana's heart.

No.

Yes.

No, I can't.

I can.

Dana's arms shook, her palms went clammy, her stomach flip-flopped. She didn't want to say the words being pushed through her heart to her tongue. She didn't even know where they came from.

Yes, she did.

She opened her mouth and the words reverberating through her flew out. "Stacy, you will be okay. But only if you're forgiven."

Stacy looked up with wide eyes. "But I don't know if Jeremy will ever forgive me."

"Not Jeremy. God."

"God?"

She covered Stacy's hands holding the balled up tissue. "Yes. As hurt as Jeremy is, God is the one whose rules you broke. Jeremy may forgive you. He may not. But God is always willing."

Stacy hiccupped again. "Someone else said something like that to me recently." She looked away. "I don't know."

"I'm not the perfect example. I haven't exactly talked about God or lived like I know Him, but a long time ago He forgave me."

"You? What would you need forgiving for? You're perfect." She snorted.

Dana stifled an ironic laugh. Perfect. She was far from it and that became clearer every day. "I'm not perfect. And it's not the specific thing that God forgives. He forgives anything. Lying, stealing, selfishness … murder."

Hope shone on Stacy's face. Then it darkened. "It sounds too easy. Too simple."

"It is."

"But don't I have to do something?"

"Yes. Believe that Jesus is God's only Son. That He is Lord and all He wants is you."

"Now you sound like one of those crazy guys that stand on the corners in Houston."

Dana smiled. "They may sound crazy, but it's true. Jesus is God's Son and died to pay for all the things we do wrong."

Stacy gazed down the hall towards Jeremy's room. She sighed and pulled her hands away. "It's a nice story, Dana. And thanks for trying to help." She stood. "God wouldn't do that for me."

She followed Stacy to the door. "He would and he did. Promise you'll think about it."

Stacy turned and gave her a quick hug. "I will." She opened the door and straightened her shoulders.

Bo stood by Stacy's car.

"You finally leaving? Good. Get off my property and don't

ever come back."

"You don't own me, Bo Singer. And you don't own this property. Your parents do and Jeremy lives here. It's up to him whether I come back or not."

He opened her door and stepped out of the way so she could climb in. Then he leaned down and said something. Dana walked closer, straining to hear. She couldn't make out a single word over the engine. Bo closed the door and stood with his arms crossed.

"What'd you say?"

"Nothing. I simply encouraged her not to come back, in terms she'd understand."

She longed to know what he'd said. One look at his set jaw and she knew she'd never be able to pry it out of him. He kept a secret like he held onto a bull.

Stacy turned her car around and peeled out, kicking up dust as she flew down the gravel lane and out of sight.

~ * ~

She hated him. He was probably the reason Jeremy wouldn't take her back. Stacy punched the gas. She'd lost everything now. For good.

Maybe she could have had him back. Maybe if he hadn't had the accident. Tears sprang to her eyes. She'd only wanted to make him jealous. If he saw her with someone else, he'd remember what they were like together and want her back. He should have been madly jealous and demanded she dump Stu and come back to him.

But no. He'd almost gotten killed. And he hated her.

A thud brought Stacy's attention back to the road. *What was that?*

She didn't see anything. Probably some random root or big rock. Their gravel lane was long and awful. A silver car came around the corner and swerved over into a spot where there were no trees as she flew by.

Stacy let off the gas. She was gonna kill somebody. She snorted. Somebody else.

A tear spilled down her cheek. She'd messed up everything. She tapped her breaks to slow down even more. She didn't want to leave the Singers' property for the last time. Not really.

If only things had been different. If only she hadn't gotten pregnant.

But she had. She had ruined everything and no one could forgive her.

God will.

Dana's words bounced around in her head. Others had said the same thing.

Maybe it was true. Maybe God would forgive her if she asked.

She pressed the brake again as she headed towards the end of the lane. She hated leaving. And she hated turning left onto a busy four-lane highway. It always made her nervous.

She pushed the brake harder, but nothing happened. Her heart raced.

Oh God. What's wrong?

She pumped the brake. Nothing.

Panic surged through her. Her stomach tightened and throat constricted.

Oh, God, forgive me! I'm sorry. I believe. Help me.

Stacy pumped the pedal again. It didn't respond and she coasted out of the driveway. A horn blew and she looked to her left. An eighteen-wheeler barreled towards her.

Her heart thudded in her ears, drowning everything else out.

God, no!

Chapter 10

Dana stared at the dust stirred up by Stacy's peal-out. As the dirt settled a tiny silver car drove up. Kara. Good. She'd lighten things up and lift Jeremy's spirits.

Kara stepped out of the tin can, as they fondly called her car. "Was that Stacy flying out of here?"

"Yeah. She came to check on Jeremy. It didn't go well."

"Apparently not. I barely had time to pull over and avoid getting hit."

Dana wrapped her friend in a hug and headed towards the house. "Let's not talk about Stacy. I'm glad you're here. Let's go cheer Jeremy up."

Metal crashed and screeched in the distance and Dana stopped short of the first step. Her heart leapt to her throat and her hand flew to her mouth. She looked wide-eyed at Kara. "What was that?"

Meeting Dana's gaze, Kara blinked, then slowly turned towards the gravel driveway.

Bo appeared at the edge of the path leading towards the barn. Dana couldn't see his face. Couldn't read his body language. Silence surrounded her and threatened to swallow her up.

A horse whinnied and she grabbed Kara's arm, dragging her back to her car. "Let's go. We have to see. Bo, come on, we might need you."

Kara sank into her seat and dropped her keys. On the third try, she got her key in the ignition. Dana stood by the passenger door waiting on Bo to move.

"Bo, Come on. We have to go." She stuck her head in the car. "Kara, call 911." Kara stared at her. "Get your phone out. Even if it's not Stacy, somebody's been in an accident. We need to call."

Kara shook her head as if shaking off cobwebs. She dug in her back pocket for her phone and flipped it open.

Dana looked over the car's roof. "Are you coming or what?"

Bo glanced her way for the first time since the blood-stopping crash. "Yeah." He trotted to the car and crawled into the backseat.

She climbed in and slammed the door.

"No, I didn't see it. We heard it. 12486 Millers Lane." Kara cranked the engine and ground the gears twice before the car slipped into reverse.

"I'm sure. Nothing else could have made that noise." The car lurched towards the lane. "Oh." Wide eyes looked at Dana. Kara covered the mouth of the phone. "Someone else is calling it in." She steered around potholes and the occasional tree root sticking up. "Thank you." She ended the call.

Dana glanced back at Bo. He stared out the front window, but she couldn't read him. What is that look? Fear? Anger? Satisfaction?

Her heart thumped loudly. She swallowed the lump in her throat. He wouldn't be happy if it was Stacy. Would he?

He hated Stacy, no doubt. But could someone who loved her so much be that cold? Did he really despise Stacy that much?

She turned to stare out the side window. Threatening tears filled her eyes and her nose burned. *Oh, God. Don't let it be Stacy. Let her be okay.*

Maybe it was a coincidence, the crash only minutes after Stacy sped away from the Singers' house.

She tried to swallow, the baseball size lump making it difficult. A tear slid down her cheek.

Kara stopped at the end of the lane. Several cars filled the highway on both sides. A few crept by in the middle two lanes. To their right, an eighteen-wheeler was stopped in the road, it's trailer at an angle behind its cab. In front of the cab, there sat a jumbled mess that looked like it had once been a yellow car.

"Oh, God. No!"

Kara's questioning, tear-filled eyes met Dana's.

"We have to go see. Maybe…" She choked up. Maybe what? No one could be alive in the middle of that tangled mess. No one.

Kara turned the car and crept towards the accident. She pulled onto the shoulder behind three other cars. Dana opened her door and blindly walked towards the gathering crowd. Sirens blared in the distance, growing louder as she moved closer.

Maybe it was just the back end of the car. Maybe she was okay. Maybe…

She cleared the part of the truck that had been blocking her view and her knees buckled.

An arm wrapped around her waist, catching her before she fell. She looked up in to Bo's dark amber eyes. His face blurred as her tears flowed freely.

Kara grabbed her other arm and stood beside her, whimpering. A fire truck pulled up, followed by an ambulance and three police cars. They allowed a police officer to push them back with the rest of the crowd as the firemen gathered around the car. They looked as helpless as Dana felt.

Words swirled around her.

"Jaws of life."

"Such a shame."

"A tragedy."

"She just pulled out. It didn't look like she even tried to stop."

"Was it just one person?"

Dana's eyes drew to an officer talking to a bulky man holding a cowboy hat in trembling hands.

He must be the driver.

She stepped forward, straining to hear what he said. The officer closest to onlookers took a step towards her, his presence stopping her from moving farther forward. His face softened when she met his gaze. He stepped closer.

"Was she a friend of yours?"

"I...we…" She looked at Bo and then Kara. Her gaze fell to the ground. "Yes."

"I'm so sorry. Did you see the accident?"

"No. We…my boyfriend lives up the lane." She waved her hand behind her towards Bo's driveway. "We were at the house." She swayed and Bo's arm tightened around her waist.

Dana steadied herself. "We heard the crash. She'd just left. We hoped it wasn't her." A fresh wave of tears burst through and she buried her head in Bo's chest. She squeezed Kara's hand as it moved to grip hers. Kara's sobs broke through the ringing in Dana's ears.

Words swirled again.

"I'm sorry."

"Poor things."

"Such a shame."

"Dead on impact."

Dana flinched as a chainsaw started up. As metal tore into metal she kept her head buried and tightened her grip on Kara's hand.

What seemed like hours later, Dana, Kara, and Bo climbed back into the little silver car. This time, Bo took the keys and drove them back up the lane.

They crept past the familiar bends and dips. The house came into view and Bo inched the car into its previous parking spot. No one moved.

He reached for Dana's hand. "I have to go tell him."

"Do you want me to come?"

"No."

Dana pushed open the passenger door. Bo's clicked shut as Kara climbed out of the backseat. He walked towards the house like a bull heading to the slaughter house. Dana and Kara clung to each other and bawled.

Moments later, the front door swung open. Jeremy wheeled himself out the door and down the ramp that had been built in the days before he came home from the hospital. She couldn't see his face. It angled down at the ground before him and his cowboy hat sat low, hiding his eyes.

He pushed the wheels with all his strength across the yard and towards the barn.

Bo stood in the doorway, his arms folded and his eyes following his brother.

She didn't know what to do. Stay or go? Bo's stoic

expression didn't provide an answer.

"What…what'd he say?"

"Nothing. Not a word."

"Think he'll be okay?"

"Eventually." Bo pulled his hat lower.

Dana looked at her friend, weeping silently beside her. How could she do this? Be there for Bo. Be there for Kara. Not collapse.

"Oh, God, help me," she muttered.

Kara grasped her hand. Panic surged through her. She glanced at Bo. His eyes were fixed on the spot where Jeremy had disappeared. Good. At least he hadn't heard her.

She squeezed Kara's hand and then let it go. She slid next to Bo and laid a hand on his arm. His empty eyes met hers.

"What do you want me to do?"

"Do?"

"Should I stay?

His shoulders slumped. "No. I don't think so. Jeremy won't want anyone here when he comes back."

"Okay. I'll call you later." She leaned up and kissed him. His expression didn't change, but he did return her kiss before heading back to the house.

She turned to her friend. "What're you going to do?"

Kara wiped the tears from her cheeks. "I don't know. I don't want to go home."

"Me either." She flipped her phone open. "It's almost six. I'm really hungry."

"You know, me too." Kara's eyes filled again. "Is that wrong? Stacy's dead and I'm hungry."

Dana cleared her throat. She glanced at the house, then back at Kara. She hooked her hands in her back pockets. "I know. It doesn't seem right. But can we do anything?" Another tear escaped down her cheek.

"No. I suppose not. I just wish…" Kara's eyes glistened.

"Me, too."

Kara walked to the driver's side of her car and slid into her seat. Dana followed.

"Where should we go?"

"I don't know. Everything's so jumbled."

"Yeah. What about Chick-fil-A? That's always good."

Kara stuck her keys in the ignition and the open door alarm

buzzed. "Okay. I'll meet you there."

She followed Kara slowly down the lane. The traffic, fire trucks, police cars, and Stacy's car were gone. Some glass had been swept to the side of the road. Her eyes filled.

Would she ever be able to pull out of here again without crying?

Silence greeted her question.

She pulled onto the highway after checking both ways three times.

God, I don't understand. Why did Stacy have to die?

Thoughts and questions pinged in Dana's mind like a pinball. Should she have said something different? What if she'd kept her longer? Talked to her more? What if Bo hadn't been so mean?

Her head ached as she pulled into the fast food restaurant's parking lot. She swiped the latest tears off her cheeks and got out to meet Kara.

She looped her arm through Kara's and stopped. She should have called Crystal. Why hadn't she thought about calling Crystal?

"What?"

She shook her head. It would have to wait for later. They pushed open the door.

Her brain felt like it'd been put in a blender and turned on 'mush'.

With a tray of piping hot food in hand a few minutes later, Dana grabbed a handful of ketchup and wove through the crowd to find an empty table.

The food was always good, but the crowd was excessive.

Kara plopped her tray down. "What's going on?"

"I don't know." Dana stuffed a ketchup-laden waffle fry in her mouth. She looked around the restaurant and stopped mid-chew.

Katherine sat across the room with three other people from the Sunday school class Dana had visited. The teacher and some other kids sat at the next table.

That's right. She vaguely remembered something about a youth progressive dinner. What were the chances that she and Kara would have ended up at the right restaurant at the right time?

She swallowed as Katherine's gaze met hers. Katherine's

smile widened and she waved.

Dana lifted her hand and attempted a grin, but a new wave of tears took over instead. Her hands flew up to shield her face from all the pairs of eyes now staring at her.

Chapter 11

"I can't believe she's dead."

Dana looked at Katherine, then at the other faces encircling her. Hunter, Emma, Gillian, Aaron, Bethany, and Pastor John surrounded her. There were others, but she couldn't remember their names.

Dana had sobbed through the story. Hand after hand had reached out to comfort her.

"Oh no."

"How awful."

"O, Lord, watch over her parents."

And the occasional sniffle surrounded her as she spoke.

Did they know what Stacy had done? The rumor mill had been flying around school for months. Surely they'd heard them. She didn't think any of the Sunday school crowd had been friends with Stacy. Still, they seemed to care.

Bethany slumped in the chair opposite Dana. "We…" She sniffled. "We'd been praying for her." She looked around at her friends. "I even tried to talk to her about God a couple weeks ago."

Her eyes widened. "You? It was you?"

"What do you mean?" Pastor John, seated in the seat to Dana's right, interjected.

"She said other people had told her about God. That He

wanted to forgive her."

"You talked to her about God?"

She blew her nose into a napkin. "Right before the accident."

"Well, that's good. How did she take it?"

She shrugged. "She was so angry. So hurt. So lost."

Pastor John sighed. "We'll never know then, whether she believed what you said or not." He folded his hand together on top of the table. "But, at least you did what you could."

Had she?

He glanced at his watch. "Listen, we're supposed to have two more stops, but I don't think anyone else is going to meet up with us." He looked around. "Hunter, why don't you and Aaron go to the next couple of spots on the schedule and the rest of us will take Dana and Kara back to the church."

"To the church?" She raised her eyebrows. "No, I should… I mean, shouldn't I go home?"

"I'm not sure it's good for you to be alone. Is there someone at home to talk to?"

Her parents were at a hospital event. They wouldn't be home until after midnight. She shook her head. "No. No one's home."

"It's settled then. We'll go back to the church." He stood and scooted his chair back. The crowd dispersed to take care of their trash and grab their things.

She stood. "You're coming, right?"

Kara scrunched her nose. "I don't know. Church? It's not really my thing."

"It hasn't really been my thing lately either. But now, I don't know where else to go."

"Chet's having a party tonight."

Dana rolled her eyes and slid her hands into her back pockets. "Yeah. That's *exactly* where I want to be."

The edges of Kara's lips turned up. "I guess not."

"You ready?" Pastor John stood next to Dana.

"I'm ready. Kara?"

"No, I don't think so. I promised Brooke I'd meet her later."

Dana squeezed her friend in a hug. "Call me tomorrow." She had a feeling, if Kara went to the party, she'd be getting tons of calls the next day.

~ * ~

Dana slid into her car, pulled out her phone, and tapped off a text to Crystal. *"Meet me @ Christ Community. NOW!"*

Her brain had found its 'on' switch now that she'd spilled the whole ugly mess of the day. Well, not the whole ugly mess, but what they needed to know.

She started her car and her phone buzzed.

"Now? I'm w/Max."

"Pls. Trust me."

"What's up?"

"Not txt. Meet me."

"K."

She slid her phone into her pocket and put her car in gear. Fifteen minutes later she parked next to a dozen or so cars in the back parking lot of Christ Community Church. Pastor John stood outside the annex building where the youth met and held events.

"I called our senior pastor. He's on his way. Do you know if Stacy's parents went to church anywhere?"

She shook her head. She'd never heard Stacy even utter the word 'church.' "No. I don't think they did."

"Do you know where she lived?"

"I could tell you how to get there, but I don't know her address."

He nodded at a group of kids walking in the door. He held the door open. "Let's go get some paper and you can write the directions down."

Dana followed him to a room with sofas, bean bag chairs, and a big screen TV. She took the pen and notepad he grabbed from a desk in the corner. She scribbled directions as best she could remember them as more students sauntered in.

There wasn't the usual loud banter and joking she'd experienced the times she'd come to Sunday school. Everyone spoke in hushed tones.

She handed the pen and paper back to Pastor John.

"Thanks." He turned his attention to the others. "All right everyone. Grab a seat. We'll start with prayer, then we'll talk."

She sat on the faded green sofa, flanked by Bethany and

Emma. Each of them grabbed one of her hands.

"Lord, we come to You with heavy hearts. In the midst of the tragic and sudden death of Stacy Athens, we bring our sorrows, doubts, and guilt to You. We don't know where she stood with You. Only You know whether she found faith in You or not at the end of her short life.

"Comfort our hearts at this time and give us the right words to say to those who are grieving deeply. Show us how You want to work in and through this tragedy by showing Your mighty hand of mercy and grace. Amen."

Mercy. Grace. Death. Those words didn't fit together. Yet, Dana felt more at peace than she had since she saw Stacy's mangled car hours earlier.

Had it been only hours? It seemed like days.

Chapter 12

Pastor John interrupted Dana's thoughts. "Who would like to start?"

Bethany raised her hand. "I didn't know Stacy that well, but we had a couple of classes together. I'd heard the rumors lately. About her and Jeremy. I thought maybe I could get her to come to church. To get her to accept God's love after she–"

"Thank you, Bethany. But remember we don't need to talk about any specifics of what anyone else has done. That's theirs to share or not. Even if they're dead."

Bethany's cheeks flushed.

Pastor John glanced at a tall, thin man standing in the doorway. "Daniela, can you monitor the sharing for a moment?"

The petite redhead nodded.

He stood. "Dana, do you mind coming with me?"

Pastor John led her into the hallway.

"Dana, this is our senior pastor, Pastor Ron."

"Nice to meet you, Dana." He held out his hand. "I'm sorry it's under these circumstances. I'm sorry for the loss of your friend."

She shook his hand, but didn't correct him about Stacy being her friend. They had, after all, been close once. Two girlfriends of two brothers who were best friends.

"Thank you."

"Dana's written down directions to the Athens' house. I believe it's Stacy's mom and step-dad." He raised his eyebrows at Dana.

She nodded.

"Okay, thanks. I'll head over now."

"You're going to her house?"

Pastor Ron's eyes crinkled when he smiled. "Yes. Her parents are going to need a lot of support."

"But you don't even know them."

The pastor's smile widened. "That's what we do. We love others even if they don't love us. Even if we don't know them."

She stared. She'd never seen such a thing in her life. The pastor at her parent's church back home didn't even know them by name. She never heard of him visiting people when someone died. He just did the services.

"Okay, then. I'll let you get back to the others. I'll see you in the morning, John." His looked at Dana. "And hopefully, I'll see you and your parents, too."

"Yes, sir."

Dana turned to follow Pastor John back in the room, but stopped when her phone buzzed. She read the text from Crystal.

"I'm here. Where ru?"

She clicked off her reply. *"N back. B right there."*

She looked up to tell Pastor John she'd be right back, but he'd already taken his seat. She tiptoed down the hall and out the glass doors. Crystal came around the corner, her long brown hair shimmering under the street lights illuminating the parking lot. Max trailed behind her.

"Okay. What's the big emergency?"

Another bout of the endless tears sprung in Dana's eyes. "Crystal, there was an accident."

"What happened?" Her eyes grew wide. Her hand came to her throat. "Was it Jeremy? Bo?"

"No." She gulped. "Stacy."

"Stacy? I don't get it."

A tear slid down Dana's cheek. "She came to see Jeremy. It didn't go well. Bo was angry. She tore down their lane and her car was hit by a truck when she tried to turn onto the highway."

Crystal stared. "How bad was it? Is she in the hospital?"

Dana shook her head as more tears flowed.

"She's not…" Crystal grabbed Max's hand, glancing at him. "She's okay, right?"

She shook her head again, averting her eyes from Crystal's gaze.

"Oh, Dana. I feel awful. And you were there? You saw it?"

She stared at her feet and nodded as Crystal's stepped forward and wrapped her arms around her.

The best friends stood in a hug until Max cleared his throat.

"So what's going on? Why're you here?"

She wiped her eyes. "I, Kara and I had to get something to eat and ran into the Sunday school class at Chick-fil-A."

"*The* Sunday school class?" Crystal stood back and folded her arms.

Dana's cheeks warmed. She hadn't told Crystal about coming to church with her parents. "Yeah. I've been coming for a while. You've been kind of busy." She nodded at Max.

"I have. But still, how could you keep from your best friend that you've been going to church? Your best friend who's been begging you to go to church with her forever?"

"It just happened."

"Yeah, well. We'll talk about that later. What's going on in there?"

"Talking. Praying. Stuff like that."

"Sounds good to me. Let's go." Crystal grabbed Max's hand and nudged Dana to lead them inside.

She paused at the doorway, listening to a girl she didn't know talk about losing her older brother in a car accident.

When she finished, Pastor John glanced up. "Good, I thought you'd left. Come on in." He motioned to the sofa, where Bethany moved to the floor and Emma scooted over.

~ * ~

"So, we'll be talking about this going to church and not telling your best friend thing."

"Yeah, yeah. I hear ya." Dana rolled her eyes, relieved to be talking about something other than the accident. She unlocked her car.

"I'm glad you called."

Dana hugged her friend. "Me, too. Thanks for coming." She looked over at Max. "Sorry to interrupt your date."

"No problem. The other option was Chet's and drama."

She searched his face. Was he serious? He and Chet were supposed to be great football buds.

Crystal grinned, her eyes twinkling.

Had church-going, straight-laced Crystal reformed where's-the-next-party Max?

"I'll call you tomorrow. After church."

Dana opened her door. "Okay. Thanks again."

"Sure."

She started her car and checked her phone. Three missed calls. Twelve texts.

Bo. *"Where ru? Why r u not answering?"*

Brooke. *"OMG. Just heard. How r u?"*

Jill. *"I can't believe it. Call me."*

She scrolled through the rest. There was one more from Bo. All the others were people asking about Stacy and the accident.

Peace filled her heart. She didn't want to talk to all the gossip-mongers about the accident. Let them find out from someone else.

The church group hadn't trash talked Stacy or begged for juicy details. Instead, they'd prayed for her family, friends, and Jeremy. Prayed. She shook her head, still amazed.

She replied to Bo's text. *"Ran n2 some friends. Txt u when I'm home."*

More questions would come. He'd want to know what friends and where. But it didn't really matter. In view of Stacy's death, she'd lost her fear of telling Bo about being at church. It was becoming too important. She'd let it slip for too long. Been angry at the wrong person for the wrong reason for too long.

Had she not moved, Bo wouldn't be in her life. Maybe God did know more than her.

She didn't understand about Jeremy's accident, or Stacy's either. But she was beginning to understand that God's character remained good even when awful things happened.

Dana waited impatiently at a long stop light. She checked her phone.

"K."

She hit clear. The clock read eleven-thirty. How in the world had it gotten so late? She'd always thought of church things as boring and had always found much better ways to spend her time.

Tonight had been different. But eleven-thirty?

The light turned green and Dana released the brake.

Let my parents not be home. No more talking. I can't take it.

She pushed the button and the garage door opened. Her shoulders dropped with relief. Her dad's car wasn't there.

"I'm home. Call me," she shot off to Bo.

Dana had made it to the bathroom before her phone buzzed. "Hewo?" She answered with a mouth full of toothpaste.

"Dana?"

"Juf sec."

She finished brushing. "Hey. Sorry about that. I'm whooped. Trying to get ready for bed."

"Yeah. I actually dozed."

"How's Jeremy?"

"Quiet. But angry, I think."

"Angry?"

"At himself. He blames himself."

"But it wasn't his fault. It wasn't anybody's fault." Was it?

"I know that."

She crawled under her covers and pulled them over her head.

"So, where were you that you couldn't answer the phone?"

"I told you. I ran into some friends. Kara and I were starving and went to Chick-fil-A."

"And you were there until eleven?"

"No." She hesitated. It was easier to be brave in her head.

"So, where were you?"

She took a deep breath. "At church."

"At church? Don't kid me, Dana. I'm not in the mood."

"I'm not kidding. The friends I met were from Sunday school. We went back to the church."

"For what? And what do you mean friends from Sunday school?"

"Bo, I'm tired. Can we talk about this tomorrow?"

"Have you gone all Christian on me, Dana? What's up with this? I don't need you preaching at me."

"I'm not preaching at you, Bo. I've been going to church. It's been nice. And tonight when I needed someone to talk to, they were there for me. Besides, it's not like I went out looking for them."

She hadn't. Yet she'd come across them at exactly the right time. Was that God? Her shoulders relaxed.

"…expect me to."

"Bo, I don't expect anything from you but to love me. And to let me go to sleep when I'm tired."

He sighed. She visualized jaw twitching. "Fine. But we're not done talking about this."

"I'll call you tomorrow. After-" Might as well not pour salt on the wound. "-lunch."

Dana flipped her phone closed and fell asleep with it in her hand.

Chapter 13

Dana rolled over, assaulted by the sun streaming through the slits in her blinds. Her head ached.

Stacy.

"Ohh," she moaned. Stacy was dead. Jeremy blamed himself. *I blame myself.*

She snuggled down in her covers.

"It's not anyone's fault," Pastor John had said. "Accidents just sometimes happen."

Maybe he was right. Maybe there's nothing she could have said or done to change things.

She flung her covers off. Pastor John. It was Sunday.

She slid out of bed and ambled to the shower. Half an hour later, with a sundress slipped on and makeup applied, she stepped into the kitchen as her mom poured a cup full of batter into the waffle iron. Bacon sizzled on the stove.

"Smells good."

"Thanks, Honey. There's a glass of orange juice in the refrigerator for you."

She grabbed it and took a swig. "Anything I can do?"

Her dad lowered his newspaper. Her mom stared. "Flip the bacon and stir the apples?"

"Sure." Anything to keep from talking.

Two hours later, she stepped into the youth room. Familiar faces greeted her, many from the night before.

"Hey, Dana. How are you?"

"Hey, Katherine. I'm okay. Glad to be here."

Katherine looked around. "I love it here. Everybody's different."

"Yeah. I know what you mean. I had a million texts last night." Dana rolled her eyes. "Not people showing concern, if you know what I mean. Not like here."

Katherine grinned. "Yeah. I get it."

Pastor John strolled over. "Good morning, Dana. How are you doing?"

"Good. Better than I thought. I had an awful headache this morning."

"That's understandable. We're glad you're here."

"Thanks."

"Well, we'd better get started." He walked to the other side of the room. "Okay, we'll start with prayers and praises."

"My Aunt Heather." A younger girl Dana didn't know spoke up. "She started radiation this week."

"My dad found a job," shared a curly, blond-headed boy.

"Stacy Athens's family," Katherine said.

The room grew quiet. A few of the students who hadn't been there the night before looked around confused.

Dana's eyes filled.

"Who's she?" the young girl from before asked.

"For those of you who weren't here last night, Stacy Athens was a senior at Western Plain. She was killed in a car accident yesterday."

Gasps and sniffles filled the room.

Pastor John folded his hands in front of him. "We'll finish the other prayer requests then we'll talk about whatever anyone needs to talk about."

~ * ~

Dana slid into the backseat of her dad's car, hoping to get a nap after lunch without any questions. She didn't remember having ever being so tired.

"So, did you know the girl who was in the accident

yesterday?"

Oh. Dana stifled a groan. *How'd he hear about it?*

"Yes."

Her mom glanced at her dad. "Stacy, didn't they say her name was?"

"Yes. Athens, I think."

Her mom twisted in her seat. "So you knew her?"

She nodded.

Her mom turned back around and Dana sighed.

"Didn't Jeremy date a Stacy at some point? It wasn't her, was it?"

Her tear-filled eyes met her mom's returned gaze.

"Oh, honey. Why didn't you say anything?"

"I'm kind of tired of talking about it."

"You're tired…"

"I met up with the Sunday school class last night. And of course we talked about it this morning."

Her mom looked at her dad, then returned her gaze to Dana. "Well, if you need to talk, your dad and I are here."

"Okay."

Dana's phone vibrated.

A message from Bo lit the screen. *"What's up? Thought u were going 2 call."*

She clicked off her response. *"On my way home."*

"From?"

"Church."

Nothing.

Once home, she grabbed a sandwich and hid out in her room. She dialed Bo's number.

"Hello?"

"Hey, it's me." She sat at her desk.

"What's going on, Dana?"

"What do you mean what's going on?" The sandwich stared at her, daring her to take a bite.

"Church again. You're changing."

"I haven't changed. I'm just busy on Sunday mornings now."

"It's more than that. You know it."

It was. "No, it's not. Nothing's changed between us."

"I told you I don't want anything to do with church."

"I know that, Bo. And I haven't brought it up, other than to say that I've been there."

"I don't like it."

Dana laid her head to rest on her left hand.

"Get it out of your system quickly, all right?"

"There's nothing to get 'out of my system.' I used to go to church. I quit. And now I'm going again. Period."

Silence greeted her.

"How's Jeremy?"

"Tore up. Miserable. The idiot still loved her."

"I'm not surprised."

"I am. She didn't deserve his love."

"Everybody deserves love, Bo."

"I said not to preach at me."

"I'm not. I know what she did. And I know she was sorry. She said it was the biggest mistake she'd ever made."

He swore and then said, "You're right it was."

She tucked a piece of hair behind her ear. "Okay. She made a mistake. And now she's dead. Can't you let it go?"

"I'm not going to pretend I liked her because she's dead. You know me better than that."

Dana eyed her sandwich and took a bite instead of responding. She did know him better than that.

"Besides, she got what she deserved."

Dana gasped and started coughing. "You–" she coughed again. "You can't mean that."

"Why not? Isn't that what your Bible says? An eye for an eye and all that. Well, she took a life. Now she's lost hers."

Dana fought the remaining tickle in her throat. She swallowed and tried to regain control of her swirling thoughts. Bo hated Stacy, no doubt. But to think she deserved to die? Talk about overreaction. She coughed one more time.

"Bo."

"What? The Bible's only good when you want to use it?"

"But there's so much more. There's love and forgiveness and mercy. There's-"

"I certainly haven't seen that part of it."

She bit her trembling bottom lip. She wanted the thoughtful, funny Bo she'd fallen in love with. Had Stacy's mistake ruined not only her and Jeremy's relationship, but theirs too?

"Bo. I'm tired and I don't want to argue. I'm gonna take a nap. I've got a paper to work on this afternoon, so I'll see you tomorrow."

"Okay. Dana?"

Her hopes soared. Maybe he'd apologize. Say he was wrong. "What?"

"Nothing. I'll see you tomorrow."

Her heart sank. She hung up and glanced at her plate. The barely touched sandwich stared back at her. She pushed it away and glimpsed her discarded Bible on her bedside table.

Everything seemed hopeless. But the pastor had said God was a God of hope. He'd quoted something, although she couldn't remember what. She flipped to the back and looked up hope, searching for some kind of answer to her suddenly flipped sideways life.

Chapter 14

Dana sat in the sanctuary that had become familiar to her in the last month. Unlike on Sunday mornings, over half of the faces scattered throughout the room were under twenty. Classmates, friends, people she'd never seen before.

Stacy's mom, step-dad, and younger sister walked in. Soft music played as other family members followed the weeping couple and nine-year-old. The child clung to her mother's hand and buried her head in her mother's dress. Stacy's step-father followed and sat stick straight next to them on the second row. People Dana assumed were grandparents, aunts, uncles and cousins filled four rows of pews.

Pastor Ron motioned for everyone to sit. "We're here today to honor and remember Stacy Athens. Her young life was cut short in a tragic accident only days ago. I never had a chance to meet her, but in the last several days I've had a chance to sit down with Stacy's parents and her little sister, Melissa." He paused and tilted his head towards the Athens' seat with a sad smile.

"I feel like I've gotten to know this vivacious young lady who was full of life."

Dana fidgeted with the tissue in her hand. She'd hoped Bo would've given in and attended Stacy's funeral. At least he'd understood why she wanted to come. She glanced at Crystal and

Max next to her. She appreciated their support, not sure how she'd have handled the funeral alone.

She'd looked around and spotted Jeremy in the back of the church just before they'd stood for the family to come in. His jaw set, he met no one's eyes. He stared at the casket.

"At this time we'd like to invite any friends and family who'd like to share memories or stories about Stacy to do so."

Pastor Ron explained how the process would work. Those waiting to speak could move forward and wait on the front side pews.

Tears rolled down her cheeks as she listened to an aunt talk about teaching Stacy to climb trees at age four. She pulled out another tissue as a cousin shared memories of swimming in a creek behind their grandparents' property when they were younger.

Each story drew Dana in and gave her insight to Stacy. Where had things gone wrong?

She looked around the room again. This time the windows caught her attention. Scenes depicting the birth, ministry, and baptism of Jesus painted the glass. Then her gaze was drawn to the cross behind Pastor Ron. Not once had anyone mentioned God or Jesus or faith. Stacy hadn't been hostile to religious things. She simply didn't believe God could love her. Maybe she'd never heard about God's love until recently.

Dana's legs straightened. Before she could question herself or think, she arrived at the front pew. She sat and stared at the cross as three other people rose and took their turns to talk.

A girl sitting to her right elbowed her.

"What?"

The girl she faintly recognized mouthed, *It's your turn.*

Dana stood and approached the empty stage. Pastor Ron handed her a microphone as she climbed the stairs. Her hands shaking, she gripped the mic and raised it to her mouth.

What was she doing? She'd lost her mind and had no idea what to say.

Oh God, give me something to say.

She licked her lips and opened her mouth. "I haven't known Stacy as long as most of you. And I wasn't always a good friend to Stacy. But she was always a good friend to me. Stacy welcomed me right into..." She looked at Jeremy sitting in his wheelchair in the back. "She welcomed me with open arms. I was the new girl in town, but she treated me like she'd known me forever."

She pictured Stacy dragging her all around the Singers' farm, laughing and sneaking up on Bo and Jeremy in the barn. Then, Stacy's tear-streaked face on her last day flashed in her mind.

"Stacy and I hadn't hung out much the last couple months, but I did see her the day–" She swallowed the growing lump in her throat. "The day of the accident. Stacy was sadder than I'd ever seen her." Should she have said that in front of her parents? She swallowed again and tucked a piece of hair behind her ear. "But she also had a glimpse of hope. Like I said, I hadn't always been a good friend to Stacy, but that day we talked about God. About His love and forgiveness."

Dana wiped her eyes with her balled up tissue. "I don't know if she talked to God or accepted His love that day, but I do know she reminded me I hadn't always done a good job of loving." She looked at Stacy's parents. Her step-dad stared straight ahead. Her mom met Dana's gaze. "Maybe that's her legacy. To remind us to forgive each other and love each other. To help us remember not to waste time and push God out of our lives. Maybe."

She stepped from behind the podium, then handed the mic back to Pastor Ron as her wobbly legs took her down the steps.

She ignored Crystal's inquisitive look as she sat. Pastor Ron stood where he did when Dana handed him the microphone. No one else came forward. Seconds later, music began and she joined the others in singing the words printed on the screen up front.

"You are my everything, all I will ever need. God let my life glorify, my words exemplify, my everything be all for You."

She continued singing and glanced behind her. She couldn't see Jeremy.

Chapter 15

Dana's stomach churned as she crept up Bo's driveway.

Her heart leapt when the familiar house came into view. She steered into her regular parking spot in front of a couple of trees off to the right.

The smells of fresh cut hay greeted her when she stepped from the car. She pushed the car door closed and gazed at the house, its silence in stark contrast to the words reverberating in her head. Jeremy had disappeared before the funeral ended and she could slip away to talk with him.

He must be torn up inside.

She turned at the sound of a galloping horse. Her jaw dropped. Jeremy bounced in the saddle. She flagged him down and ran to the fence.

"What are you doing? Are you crazy?"

Jeremy patted the horse's neck and panted. "I…needed…air."

Dana shoved her hands into her back pockets. "But your leg. You're going to hurt yourself."

"I'm fine." He looked across the field.

She waited for his eyes to meet hers. "I saw you, Jeremy. I know you were there."

His jaw tightened. *Just like Bo.*

"I was there. So what?"

"It's okay to miss her." She stepped closer and put her hand on his. "It's okay."

His eyes glistened.

"I miss her, too."

A door slammed and her head snapped toward the house. Bo lumbered down the steps and across the lawn.

"What's going on here?" He draped a possessive arm over her shoulders. "You movin' in on my girl?"

Jeremy returned his younger brother's grin. "Nah. She's movin' in on me."

Bo kissed Dana below her ear. "Is that right? I'll just have to remind her how good she has it. No need to settle for second best."

"Maybe I'll show her what a real man is like." Jeremy winked.

She chuckled and snuggled against Bo reveling in the normalcy of the brothers ribbing each other.

"You trying to prove something riding that thing? Don't think your therapist would approve."

Jeremy cocked his head to the side. "No, she wouldn't. And you're not going to tell her."

"Maybe I will." Bo's eyes twinkled. "Maybe I won't. Now get off that thing and Dana and I will walk her back to the barn."

Bo hopped the fence and let Jeremy lean on him as he slid off the majestic brown mare. Jeremy landed with a groan

Dana creased her brow and she reached out as Bo helped Jeremy squeeze through the top and middle fence panels.

"I'm okay." He shook her off. He took one step and his leg buckled beneath him.

"Jeremy!" She squatted beside him and looked over her shoulder at Bo. He stood helplessly holding onto the mare's reins. "Where's the wheelchair?"

"At the barn." He pushed against the ground and ended up on both hands, one leg, and one foot. He pushed again, forcing his weight on his good leg first. One more shove and he stood upright. "I've got it." He huffed as if he'd run a marathon.

Dana gaped after Jeremy as he hobbled across the yard. She shook her head and turned to Bo. His set jaw and white knuckles gripped around the reins told her everything about the worry he held inside and refused to admit to her.

"You gonna walk this horse back to the barn with me or not?"

She nodded and stepped through the fence.

~ * ~

Dana held tight to Bo's hand as they climbed the hill leading from the barn to the yard behind his house. He'd returned the wheelchair to the house while she started on the chestnut mare. Cooling a horse down, brushing its coat, stroking its mane, always calmed her. Brought a sense of home and belonging. She was as far removed from the city life she grew up in as possible. And she loved it.

She smiled at Bo and snuck a kiss as they rounded the corner.

"I–" Dana's heart sped up and they stopped in their tracks. A police car sat at the end of the driveway. She looked up at Bo. "What in the world?"

"I don't know."

They sped up. Surely something else couldn't' have happened. They'd been through enough. She couldn't take anything else.

She followed Bo up the porch steps and through the front door.

"That's probably him." Jeremy's voice came from the den.

Seconds later they were greeted by Jeremy, stationary on the sofa, and two uniformed police officers who stood when they entered.

"Bo Singer?" The one on the left, not much older than Jeremy, sounded stiff and official.

He looked from one officer to the other. "Yeah."

"We need to ask you some questions in regard to Stacy Athens' car accident."

"Okay." He didn't move. Dana clung to his hand.

The older officer stood a few inches taller than the younger one. He scrubbed his fingers through his dark military haircut peppered with gray, cleared his throat, and looked at Dana. "Mind if we talk in private?"

Bo squeezed her hand. "Yes, I do mind. This is my girlfriend Dana. She was here that day, too. So if you need questions answered, maybe she should be here, too."

"Oh." The y`oung, formal officer spoke up. "Then we'd like to question you, too, Ma'am."

Dana's heart sped up. She never did well talking to police. Even when she knew she hadn't done anything wrong. The one time she'd gotten pulled over for a speeding ticket, she'd froze, barely getting a word out. Her hands shook as she followed Bo and sat on the couch.

Young, stiff-necked officer flipped open a notebook and clicked open a pen. "Mr. Singer, I understand you were here the day of the accident."

"I was."

"And…" he glared at Bo. "I also understand you didn't care much for Miss Athens."

He met the officer's gaze squarely. "I didn't like her at all. And I didn't think she should be here."

The shaking spread throughout Dana's body. She rubbed her free hand on the leg of her jeans. What was going on? Why were they questioning Bo about the accident?

"Your brother told us he and Miss Athens had an argument before she left and that she was upset." His pen hovered over the notebook. "Could you tell me where you were while Miss Athens was here?"

"Some of the time I was in the front yard. The rest of the time I'd gone to the barn."

"And did you have any interaction with Miss Athens?"

Bo's hand tightened around Dana's. "I told her the same thing I just told you. She had no right to be at my house."

"At any time were you alone with Miss Athens' car?" He asked the question with the calm of asking Bo what he had for breakfast.

Dana's eyes widened. They're accusing Bo of something. Stacy's death had been an accident. He didn't have anything to do with it.

"No," Bo answered in a firm voice.

Dana couldn't read anything from his expression. Had he meant to lie? She withdrew her shaking hand and clasped it with her other one, willing them to be still. He couldn't have had anything to do with the accident. He just couldn't have.

She met the gaze of older, quiet officer. He glanced at her

hands, then back to her face. He spoke up for the first time. "And what is your name, Miss? I don't think we caught it."

"Dana."

Young officer scribbled. "Dana…?"

"Little."

Quiet, kind-eyed officer took over the questioning as the younger one continued taking notes. "And you were here that day, Miss Little? The day of Miss Athens' accident."

"Yes, Sir." She focused on the warmth of Bo's body next to her, yet her hands refused to stop shaking.

Older cop smiled. "And you talked with Miss Athens?"

"Yes."

"And when was that, exactly?"

"Umm…" She racked her brain. When had she talked to Stacy? The accident had pushed everything else about that day out of her mind. "I…we…right before she left."

"That was before or after Mr. Singer spoke with her?"

"You mean Bo or Jeremy?"

His eyes crinkled as his grin widened. "I guess there are two of them, aren't there? Let's start with Jeremy."

"I spoke with her after Jeremy did."

"And she was upset?"

Dana rubbed her palms on her lap. "She was."

"Do you know what had upset her?"

She looked at Jeremy, unsure of how much to say.

Jeremy took the pressure off. "I told you before. She and I had broken up a while back and she'd come to see me after I had an accident. When she finally accepted there was no chance we'd get back together, she got upset."

"And did she say anything to you about that conversation, Miss Little?"

"Some."

"Did she say anything to you about anything else?"

Dana swallowed the lump in her throat. She needed to tell the truth. But they didn't need to know about the abortion. That didn't matter anymore. "Only that she regretted the way things happened with Jeremy and that she still loved him."

Bo stiffened beside her. He leaned back and propped his ankle on the opposite knee.

Young officer spoke up again. "And the other Mr. Singer?

Did Bo talk to Miss Athens before you did?"

She tucked a loose lock of hair behind her ear. "No. That was after."

"So, he was the last one to talk to her before the accident?"

"Yes."

"And did you hear what he said?"

"Like he said, he told her to get off the property."

"Is that all he said?"

"Yes, I–" The picture of Bo leaning down behind Stacy's car door flashed in her mind. He had said something else.

Quiet officer spoke up again. "Dana? Is there something you've remembered?"

"I…" She looked at Bo. He stared at the ceiling. "He did say something else, but I didn't hear it."

"You didn't hear it?"

She re-tucked that stubborn lock of hair behind her ear again. "He stood by her car. I was on the porch."

"He was by Miss Athens car when you came out of the house?"

Her eyes darted from Bo to the officers. "Umm. I guess he was."

Formal officer's eyes bore into Bo's. "I thought you weren't alone with Miss Athens' car."

"I wasn't. I came up from the barn right before she came out of the house. I opened her car door to help speed up her exit."

The cop scribbled more in his stupid little notebook.

Chapter 16

Dana leaned against her car and stared into Bo's eyes. She wished she could read his thoughts. She'd always trusted him, but that trust now had a crack in it.

Her hands had finally stopped shaking, although it took halfway through dinner for them to do so. Neither Bo nor Jeremy said anything to their parents about the police coming by. She wasn't quite sure what that meant. Maybe they saw it as routine, no big deal.

She did. They hadn't hidden their suspicions of Bo. That he'd done something awful.

"Hey."

She shivered under the touch of his fingers on her arm. "Hey."

"You here with me or what?"

"I'm here." He couldn't have done anything. She knew it. She tucked that stubborn lock of hair behind her ear.

"What?" Bo raised his eyebrows.

She shouldn't be so easy to read. "Why didn't you say anything to your parents?"

"About what? About the police?"

"Yeah."

Bo snorted. "There's no reason to tell them. They certainly

don't want to hear anything else about Stacy. I'm sure it's all standard. They have to ask questions after accidents."

"It didn't sound routine to me. It sounded like they don't think it was an accident."

Bo wrapped an arm around Dana and drew her close. "Nah. Why would they think anything else?"

She leaned against his chest. "I don't know."

He kissed the top of her head. "Nothing to worry about, my little trembler."

She bit her bottom lip. "You noticed?"

"How could I not? I thought you were going to shake right off the couch."

"Yeah, well, I don't like talking to cops."

"If you haven't done anything wrong, there's nothing to be afraid of."

"I know. But I still don't like it." She checked her phone. "I'm not going to like the look on my dad's face either if I don't leave now. It is a school night." She rolled her eyes

"Yes, it is. You up for breakfast in the mornin'?"

Men. Always thinking about food. "No. I've got a test to study for and the extra sleep will do me good. It's been a long day."

"Okay. I'll see you after first period."

~ * ~

Dana shoved her books in her locker and slammed it. She turned to leave and jumped when she saw Crystal standing less than two feet away.

"Good grief!"

Crystal grinned. "What's got you so jumpy?"

"Nothing. I didn't expect a pair of eyes to be staring at me when I turned around."

Crystal batted her eyelashes. "A beautiful pair, though."

She rolled hers. "I don't know. I hardly see them anymore."

Crystal blushed and looped her arm through Dana's. "I was at the funeral."

"And left right after with Max."

"I'm here now."

They squeezed through the exit door together. How she'd missed her friend. "Which begs the question: Where is Max?"

Crystal steered them to Dana's car. "He had a job interview."

"A job interview? Max?"

Crystal giggled. "Yeah. His parents said he needs a summer job."

"So I may actually get to see you this summer."

"You'll see me anyway."

"Uh huh." Dana unlocked her car door.

"So what are you up to this afternoon?"

"I hadn't really decided. Home and veg I guess."

"Mind if I join you?"

She eyed her best friend. "Everything okay at your place?"

"The same."

Crystal never talked much about home, but in the months they'd been friends Dana learned that Crystal's mom drank. A lot. Crystal never invited Dana over. The few times Dana had picked Crystal up from her house, she'd dashed out to the car like she was escaping a fire. Crystal had never said one word about her dad.

"Sure, I'd love the company."

A waving arm caught Dana's attention. She recognized Katherine's curly brown hair. She raised her hand in return and Katherine jogged across the parking lot.

"Hey," she panted. "How are you?"

"Okay."

"You sure? I heard about the police coming to Bo's house."

She bit her lower lip and looked at Crystal, whose eyes darted away. She returned her gaze to Katherine. "You heard about that?"

"Yeah. Chet saw the car leaving their driveway. It's all over school. What's going on?"

Dana looked at Crystal again. Nothing. She brushed the air as if swatting a mosquito. "Nothing. Just normal questions after the accident."

"I hope so." Katherine shifted to her other foot. "Anyway, I wondered if you had anything going on tonight. You haven't come to youth on Wednesday yet, and I thought you might like to come."

"I don't know. Crystal's coming over. And I'd have to ask my parents." Who would probably fall on the floor in shock and then shove her out the door.

Crystal raised her hands. "Don't miss out on my account. I

have to be at my church at five-thirty to help with dinner."

"Oh, well, I'll have to see."

Katherine shifted again. "Okay. I hope to see you there. We start at six."

"Thanks."

Katherine bounded off and Dana narrowed her eyes. "You knew it's going around school about the police being at Bo's and didn't say anything?"

Crystal looked around and spoke in a hushed tone. "I knew. I thought we'd talk about it at your house."

Dana chewed on her lower lip in response.

~ * ~

Dana handed Crystal a soda out of the refrigerator. They plopped on the sofa and Dana flipped the TV on. With CMT in the background, she turned to her friend and hid the quiver in her hands by playing with the tab on the can.

"So why's everyone talking about the police being at Bo's house."

"Chet has a cousin at the police station. You know how he can be. He saw the cop car pulling out and called to see what he could find out. His cousin didn't say much, but he did tell Chet they'd found some things that made them investigate the accident."

Her heart sped up. "What things?"

"I don't know. But you know how things are at Western Plain. There's a million rumors flying."

"Like what?"

Crystal stared at the TV.

Dana rubbed her clammy hands on her shorts.

Crystal looked at her. "Everybody knows Bo hated Stacy. Some people are saying he did something to her car."

Dana's hand flew to her mouth. "No!"

Crystal touched Dana's arm. "Don't worry. Nobody believes it. I've known Bo my whole life. He may have a temper, but he wouldn't do something like that."

"I know that. You know that. But…."

"It's nothing, I'm sure." She got up. "I'm hungry, let's scrounge in your kitchen and see what's there."

She trudged behind Crystal. The accusation fit with the

questions the police had asked the day before. It was ludicrous. He couldn't have done anything to Stacy's car. She pictured Bo standing by the car when they'd gone outside.

Maybe he would have had time. But, no. Even if he'd had the opportunity, Bo wouldn't purposefully put someone in danger. Not even Stacy.

She grabbed the bag of chips Crystal handed her. Bo hated Stacy. Everyone knew that. But he wasn't capable of murder. But could he have done something, as a warning, thinking she wouldn't get hurt?

She returned to the den.

"Dana."

She shook the images from her head. "What?"

"Don't worry about it. Nothing will come of it."

"I hope not."

Chapter 17

Friday. Finally.

Dana tapped her pencil on the test in front of her. Three more exams, then no more school for three whole months.

She scribbled the rest of her answer and flipped the page. Whew. Last question.

Discuss the similarities between the French and Russian revolutions. Include the main causes behind each, the precipitating events, and the effects on each economy.

Good grief.

She'd read over all her notes, and could swing this, but her muscles ached to slump over the desk and take a nap. She couldn't concentrate on revolutions that had occurred decades ago and had nothing to do with her. Her mind felt like a tennis court, with thoughts about Stacy's death and the cops coming to Bo's house bouncing around and mixing with things she'd been learning from Pastor John and the youth group.

'God has everything in control,' Pastor John had told her.

'Don't worry. Trust God,' the petite redhead in Sunday school had said.

She had no idea how to follow that piece of advice.

Pray, they told her. Read the Bible. Keep coming to Sunday school and other youth events.

It couldn't be that simple. Besides, she didn't know how to pray.

But would God answer her prayers about Bo since he didn't believe in God?

Her love and desire for Bo pulled her one direction while the peace and friendships she'd found at church tugged her in the other. She wasn't sure she could hold herself together much longer. But she couldn't give up either one.

But I love him, God. Doesn't that matter? Won't that make a difference?

Tears formed in her eyes. She couldn't imagine life without Bo.

Her teacher cleared her throat. Dana stopped tapping her pencil and met Ms. Harnett's hard gaze. She looked back down at her paper, poised her pencil above it, and bit her bottom lip.

The French Revolution, while having a much wider scope and dramatically different catalyst, also had many similarities to the Russian Revolution.

The clock ticked as Dana's pencil took on a life of its own. Her head bent down, she scribbled furiously.

In conclusion, while the French and Russian revolutions were different in many aspects, they also had several similarities. The-

A noise in the hallway caught Dana's attention. Several heads turned towards the door, straining to see through the small window. Her stomach lurched when a man walked by. It was the older, quiet officer that had come by Bo's house. Bo passed by the window next, followed closely by Young, Arrogant cop.

Her heart thudded and her hands quaked furiously. Dropping the pencil, she looked desperately around the room. Twenty-three pairs of eyes stared back at her. She slid out of her desk, wove through the rows of desks, and threw open the door, ignoring her teacher's reprimand.

"Bo."

His hands were cuffed behind his back. He and the officers stopped and looked back at her.

"What's going on?"

Bo's jaw twitched, but Dana saw something in his eyes she'd never seen before.

"It's nothing. A misunderstanding." His slumped shoulders told her he didn't believe his own words.

"It's no mistake, Ma'am. We're charging Bo Singer with the murder of Stacy Athens."

She stared as they walked down the hallway and around the corner. The shaking trekked from her hands, up her arms, and down her legs. She squeaked out one word, "No."

Then everything went black.

~ * ~

Dana blinked her eyes open. Where was she?

She looked around. A nutrition guide poster. Another poster touting the danger of drugs. A woman sat at a desk across the room, her salt-and-pepper covered head bent over paperwork.

The nurse's office.

The picture of Bo being carted off by the cops flooded her mind. She groaned.

Mrs. Zucker rose out of her chair and walked over to Dana. "You're awake." She held two fingers to her wrist. Next, she listened to her heart with the stethoscope. "Everything seems to be normal. How are you feeling?"

Tears stung Dana's eyes. "I don't know." She turned her head. "Numb."

"That's understandable. At least you didn't get hurt. If Chet hadn't caught you, you'd have dropped right to the floor and gotten a nasty bump on your head."

"Chet caught me?"

The nurse smiled. "He did. Good thing, too."

Great. She'd rather it'd been anyone but him.

"Since you seem to be doing all right, I'm going to go get Mrs. Spencer."

"Mrs. Spencer?" The guidance counselor? Did she do anything other than help with class schedules?

Well, she did try to have me come see her when I first moved here.

"Yes. Given what happened, she wanted to talk with you when you came to."

"Do I have a choice? I mean, I really want to go. I need to find Bo."

The nurse placed a hand on her arm. "Dana, there's next to no chance that you'll get to see Bo today. Maybe not for several days. I think it would be good for you to talk with someone."

Dana closed her eyes and chewed on her bottom lip. She didn't want to talk with just someone. She wanted to talk with Bo. "Do I have to?"

"Of course you don't. But will you just see what she has to say?"

"I guess."

"Good. Give Mrs. Spencer a few minutes. By then your parents should be here to pick you up."

She sat up and her head spun. "My parents? You called my parents?" That means she couldn't even get her head straight before being bombarded with a million questions.

"Yes. It's standard when a student passes out."

And how often does that happen? Dana wanted to snap.

"I'll make sure Mrs. Spencer is ready for you. I'll be right back."

When the nurse exited, Dana swung her legs off the side of the table. What was she going to do? How could they think Bo would do such a thing?

The venomous words she'd heard Bo spout when talking about or to Stacy swam in her head. He hated Stacy. No one doubted that. But he wouldn't commit murder. She just knew he wouldn't.

Right?

Chapter 18

Dana rolled over and tucked her head under the covers to block the light coming through her window. Her eyelids felt heavy, drooping each time she opened them.

She felt drugged.

But no, she hadn't been drugged. Her emotions had been put in a blender and pulverized. Mrs. Spencer had seemed nice and genuinely concerned, but Dana couldn't remember a word she'd said. Still, a glimmer of hope had pierced the darkness the sight of Bo in handcuffs had created.

The ride home with her parents had done its best to squash that tiny speck of hope. Question after question after question. Most she didn't have answers to.

'Why would the police think Bo had something to do with the accident?'

'The police came to Bo's house and questioned him? Why didn't you tell us?'

'They questioned *you*?'

Dana's eyes welled up with tears. She tossed the covers off her head. Her bedside clock read six-forty.

A.m. or p.m.?

Blinking, she reached for her cell phone and dialed Jeremy's number for the umpteenth time.

Please answer. Please, please answer.

By the third ring, she'd given up.

"Hello," Jeremy's deep, twangy voice answered.

"Jeremy, what's going on? Where's Bo? Please tell me this is a joke. That they got it all wrong."

He sighed. "I wish. My folks and I are heading home from the police station. It's real. They questioned him for like three hours. They're sending him to juvi. They can keep him there until the trial."

"No." She fell back onto her pillow and covered her eyes with her free hand. "This can't be happening. It's crazy."

Silence echoed across the line.

"So what happens next? Can I see him?"

"We're not sure exactly. He's got a public defender and my parents have an appointment to meet with him tomorrow. Every lawyer they called wanted a few thousand dollars retainer."

She waited, ignoring the beep that notified her of a new message.

"My parents don't have that kind of money sitting around. The farm's almost paid off, so they can refinance, but that could take a month or longer."

"Oh, Jeremy I'm so sorry. There's got to be something I can do."

"Not now. Except…"

"What? Anything."

"Well…what you said at the funeral. Do you believe it?"

"I do."

"Then pray. Hard."

She swallowed the lump that suddenly took up residence in her throat. "I will."

He sighed. "Thanks, Dana."

"I'll call you tomorrow. What time's your parent's appointment?"

"Ten, I think."

"Okay, I'll call you after lunch. And if you talk to Bo, tell him I love him and believe in him."

"I will."

She closed her phone and flipped it back open to read the newest text.

"Where r u & what's going on? Why won't u answer me?"

Crystal.

"Been asleep. Tlkd 2 J."

Her phone sang almost immediately.

"Hey. Why haven't you been answering me? I'm worried sick."

"Sorry. I fell asleep after I got home. It's been the longest day of my life."

"Is it true? Did they really arrest Bo for murdering Stacy?"

Dana winced. The words linking him to murder pierced her heart again. "Yes," she whispered. "It's true, but I have no idea why. It was an accident. We were all there."

"Yeah. I'm so sorry."

"Thanks." She played with a lock of hair then tucked it behind her ear.

"What are you doing tonight?"

She scoffed. "I was going to go to the rodeo. Now I guess I'll stay home and avoid my parents."

"No. That won't do. You are not throwing yourself a pity party. Come out with Max and me."

"That's exactly the thing I need to top off my day, to be the third wheel on your date."

"Come on. It'll be fine."

Dana's phone beeped and she glanced at the incoming text.

"Watching movie @ church 2nite @7. Pls come!"

"I'm good, really."

"You're not fine. I know you better than that."

Dana typed a quick response. *"Mayb."*

"Well, I will be okay. I need to grab some dinner, then maybe I'll hunker down with a movie."

"Not acceptable. I'm not leaving you to wallow in your tears."

She rolled her eyes. If everyone would just leave her alone.

"Katherine texted me that they're watching a movie at church."

"Great. Promise you'll go and I'll leave you alone."

"Promise," Dana muttered.

"Okay. But I'll be checking up on you. I got Katherine's number at school today. I'm sending her a message right now telling her you'll be there and to let me know if you don't show."

She heard the tap-tap and got up. "Fine. I'm going. I'm

changing right now." She slipped off her lavender tank top and rummaged in her closet for something fresh and appropriate. She settled on a red t-shirt she'd gotten for her birthday from her parents and never worn before.

"So, you're going to church?"

Her phone beeped. "Yes. I'm heading to the bathroom to brush my hair. Do you really want a play-by-play?"

"Good." Satisfaction filled Crystal's voice. "I'll call you tomorrow. Or better yet, I'll come over."

"Max working?"

"I'm not answering that, smart aleck."

"Okay. I should be here. I'm hoping to go see Bo after lunch."

"They'll let you?"

Her insides bounced around like they were riding a bucking bronco. The hand holding her brush fell to her side. "I don't know. I hope so."

"I'll come by after breakfast. No, *for* breakfast. You're mom's the best cook."

Her lips turned up. "Yeah, she is. And I don't think she has anywhere to go in the morning."

Crystal said good-bye and Dana checked her new text message.

"Cu @ 7. Don't eat. Lots of food!"

She sighed. *"K."*

She couldn't quite decide whether having a stubborn best friend was beneficial or not.

Dana pulled the brush through her hair and examined her reflection. She was going to have to work extra hard to cover up those bags. She threw her brush in the drawer and stared at her makeup. Who really cared? It wasn't like anything remained secret in the tiny town. She slammed the drawer shut and jumped at a rap on the door.

"Yes?"

"Dana? It's mom."

It couldn't be anyone else.

"Are you okay?"

She swung the door open. "I'm okay, I guess."

"You going out?"

"Yeah, Katherine invited me to a movie at church."

Relief filled her mom's face. "That's fine if you're going to church. I thought you might want to talk, though."

She slid her hands into her back pockets. "Mom, I'm kinda talked out. There's nothing I can do. Jeremy didn't even really know anything."

"You talked to Jeremy?"

"A little while ago. His parents are meeting with a public defender tomorrow."

"A public defender? What about their lawyer?"

She scrunched up her nose. "They don't have a lawyer, Mom. They can't even afford the retainer for one. Jeremy said they're talking about mortgaging the farm, but that could take forever."

Her mom's hand flew to her mouth and her eyes grew round as pancakes. "No, they can't do that. They need someone who doesn't have a hundred other cases. Someone who can really help Bo."

Her shoulders relaxed. Her mom believed in his innocence. At least that's a start. "They don't have a choice."

Dana's mom put her hands on her hips. She recognized the determination in her face and suppressed a grin. The gears were working, and that usually meant nobody had better get in the way. "We'll see about that."

She pecked her mom's cheek. "Thanks, Mom."

"For what?"

"For not making me stay here and answer a thousand more questions." She breathed in and out deeply. "And for believing in Bo."

"Bo's not exactly what your father and I pictured for you, Dana. But murder? It's preposterous."

Chapter 19

Dana stared at her ceiling, moonlight illuminating the gold light fixture in the center. The words from the movie, the songs, the determination, the scene of seeing Bo hauled off by the cops all fought for her attention. The movie had shown how to believe even when hope seemed to vanish like a snowball in July.

Her boyfriend had been accused of murder, but she knew he hadn't done it. She sat up. The tune of a song from the night before kept reverberating in her mind, but she couldn't remember all the lyrics.

Throwing off her covers, she crossed her room in two swift steps, and punched her laptop's power button. A few keystrokes later she found herself listening to the song that held the words eating at her.

"When the world has flipped around and you can't get your feet on the ground, when the sun refuses to shine, don't give up, give in, but give it over to Him. Be still and believe He who is love has the best in store for you. Close the world out and then you will hear the melody of Truth."

As the song played for the fourth time, she sank to her knees.

"Oh, God," she moaned. "I want to believe. I do. I don't know how. It seems impossible."

Head hanging, hands on her knees, she sat still. Waiting for an answer. Waiting to wake up from this terrible nightmare.

Instead, her computer pinged, notifying her of a new instant message.

She looked up and saw Crystal's name in the IM box. Scooting back to the chair, she read the message. "What r u doing up?"

"Couldn't sleep."

"Me either. Movie good?"

"Yeah…" Her fingers paused over the keys. She had enjoyed the movie. But now it tortured her. How did someone have faith that everything would turn out right when things stunk worse than a neglected horse stable?

"You there?"

Her unsent response sat mocking her. Blinker saying, 'Answer me. Answer me.' She let her fingers talk for her.

"Having trouble believing everything will be okay. ☹"

The next ding caught her by surprise. A new IM window popped up. "Been thinking bout u," Katherine wrote. "Felt led to share Matt. 17:20."

A ping from Crystal. "It'll b ok. I just know it. Don't lose hope."

"Thx," she responded to Katherine.

To Crystal, she typed, "Feels awfully hopeless."

Ping. "No prob. Will b praying. Night."

"Night."

Crystal again. "Just bc u can't c, doesn't mean it's not going 2 turn out ok."

Dana sighed. Her muscles begged her to lie down and sleep for a couple days. Her mind refused to rest at all. God had saved her. Had called her back to Him. But would He save Bo? He wouldn't even consider that God could be good. Any thread of belief he could have had was tainted with hatred that seared hot enough to brand.

She had nothing left to give anyone. Nothing left to say. Maybe Crystal would sign off and let her be.

Her computer chimed again and a grin snuck on her lips. She should have known better.

"Hebrews 11:1. Love u!!"

Was it preach to Dana night? "Thx. LU2."

She sat staring at the screen. She should go to bed. An aching and longing to crawl under her covers and hide pulsed with each heartbeat.

Neither of the verses rang familiar to her. Of course, she'd only gotten back into church the last couple months. Reaching almost involuntarily, she wrapped her fingers around the Bible and began flipping pages. She came to Matthew first.

"He replied, 'Because you have so little faith. Truly I tell you, if you have faith as small as a mustard seed, you can say to this mountain, "Move from here to there," and it will move. Nothing will be impossible for you.'"

Move a mountain. Bo's arrest did seem like a mountain. Faith. The churning in her stomach told her the situation was impossible. The words in front of her said different.

In a huff, she flipped more pages. She didn't want faith to be the answer. She wanted a phone call from Bo telling her he'd been released and it had all been a horrible mistake. But that hadn't happened.

Hebrews. Page by page, she turned, scouting out chapter eleven. She should have known.

"Now faith is confidence in what we hope for and assurance about what we do not see."

Faith. God wanted her to believe in what she couldn't see. Her eyes shot upwards. But this time, her gaze aimed beyond the ceiling, roof, and even the clouds she imagined floated in the sky.

"Okay. I believe Bo's innocent. I believe he'll get out of this mess. I choose to believe you."

She snapped her laptop shut and slumped into bed. Snuggled down, she yanked the comforter over her head. She pulled out Bo's shirt she kept under her pillow and inhaled his scent. Minutes later she dreamt about being in his arms, enjoying the freedom of watching the horses gallop across the field together.

~ * ~

Dana peeled her eyes open. She felt the cotton shirt still in the grip of her right hand. Waves of grief, doubt, and fear crashed over her. Bo was in jail. Charged with murder. Her head pounded and her neck ached.

Choose.

Choose. She shook her head trying to remember what it meant. Suddenly, the words that had kept her awake the night before came in surges, washing away everything else. The melody of truth. Choose to believe.

Okay, God. I choose to believe you. Make the truth be that Bo's not guilty and will get out of this.

She rolled over and inhaled the musky scent with a hint of straw and horse hair. She believed, chose to believe, but that left her feeling helpless. The hopelessness had faded, but the helplessness caught her breath and swept it away.

She'd pray. She'd believe. But there had to be something she could *do.*

Keeping a tight grip on Bo's shirt, she threw the covers back. Her Bible lay open next to her laptop. Hebrews. No, that's not it. She flipped back to Matthew, but couldn't remember which chapter. Slowly she thumbed through until the words in chapter seventeen caught her eye.

The churning in her stomach calmed. She swallowed and read the verse again. A smile crept across her lips. Believing didn't mean she had to sit around and wait. She could talk to the mountain and make it move. Not sure exactly what that meant, doubt tried to creep back in.

"No. I choose to believe. Mountain, you will move, even if I have to shove you out of the way myself."

She jumped at the rap on her door. "Dana," her mom's voice came through the painted wood, "Crystal's here. She's on her second waffle."

Great. Her mom probably thought she'd completely lost it, in her room talking to herself. Oh, well. Maybe she was a bit crazy. "Be there in a minute. I'm gonna hit the restroom first."

"Okay."

She didn't hear any movement. No footsteps down the hall.

"I'm okay, Mom, I promise. I'll be there in a few."

"Okay, dear." This time, her mom retreated.

She glanced at her Bible once more. Resolve planted itself as firm as the grip she had on Bo's shirt. She loosened her grasp on the plaid cotton and slid it underneath her pillow. She'd let go of the shirt, but her resolve to do whatever it took to clear Bo's name didn't budge even a hair.

Chapter 20

Dana's heart leapt when she saw Jeremy's number pop up on her phone. Crystal raised her eyebrow and she nodded. She hit the pause button on the remote control and the characters on the 65 inch screen across the room froze.

"Hello? Jeremy?"

"Yeah."

"How'd it go? How's Bo? Did he look okay? What'd the lawyer say?"

"One question at a time."

She forced herself to sit back against the sofa. "Okay. Sorry. How's Bo?"

"As expected, I guess. He didn't sleep well and is miserable. He doesn't understand."

"None of us do. But he's all right?"

"He'll survive."

Her heart ached. Bo must be so angry, scared. And lonely.

"Um, Dana?"

"Yeah?"

"Are your parents home?"

"My parents?"

"My mom wanted to talk to yours. Or your dad. Either one."

She shook her head. What could Bo's mom want with her parents?

"No. They're both out." She glanced at the clock. My mom said she'd be back around four."

"Okay. We should be home by then. Could you have her call?"

"Sure. But what's up?"

Jeremy sighed. "A lawyer showed up this morning. He said your parents asked him to come."

"My…" Her parents had sent a lawyer. No, way.

The determined look on her mom's face the day before popped into her mind. They really did believe in Bo's innocence. And they believed enough to pay for a lawyer. Her heart threatened to burst and she wished they were there to thank. "I didn't know."

"Yeah. He's good, too."

"So what'd he say?"

"He said the first thing that would happen is Bo will have an arraignment hearing Monday morning. That's when the district attorney presents his evidence to the judge. The judge can then decide to let Bo go home until the trial or keep him in detention."

Hope soared. "He could come home Monday?"

"Not likely. Since he's charged with first degree murder, they'll keep him in detention. Then they have three weeks to try him."

First degree? That meant they thought he planned to kill Stacy. She dropped her head back against the sofa.

And they'd know his fate in three weeks. She only had twenty-one days to clear Bo's name. Impossibility landed right on her shoulders, tightening the muscles in her neck.

The bright spot - her parents were on her side. And the lawyer actually cared.

"What's the lawyer's name?"

"Umm, Wiser, I think."

Dana typed the name in her phone. "Do you know his number?"

"No."

Of course not. He wouldn't have a reason to. "That's okay. I'll find it." She clicked save. "Can I come see Bo?" She released the question she most wanted the answer to.

"I think so. You have to be added to the list of okay'd

visitors and you have to come with an adult that's on the list."

"So, when's the next time your parents are going?"

She heard muffled voices. "Tomorrow at two."

"I'll be at your house at one."

"My–"

Dana hung up before he could finish his sentence. She didn't want to give Bo's parents a chance to say that she shouldn't go. That they didn't want her to go. No one would stop her from seeing Bo and letting him know how she felt.

Crystal's raised eyebrows greeted her. "So?"

"He's okay. I'm going with his parents to see him tomorrow. And my parents got him a lawyer."

"Get out."

She smiled. "It's true."

"Your dad got Bo a lawyer?"

"He did." It was probably more her mom, but her dad would've been the one with the contact. Maybe he cared more than he let on.

Crystal whistled. "That's awesome."

"I know." She looked over. "Jeremy said he's good. And he cares about Bo's case. At least he's not stuck with a public defender with a hundred other cases. Maybe this guy will actually fight for him."

Crystal remained silent. Dana met her gaze. "What?"

"What's gotten into you?"

"What do you mean?"

Crystal leaned forward. "You've been a wreck since Stacy died. You passed out yesterday at school when you saw Bo arrested. I thought for sure you'd be a basket case by now."

She punched Crystal's arm. "Thanks, friend."

"No, really. What's up?"

"I…I don't know. It's like God's talking to me. Telling me that He's got everything covered." And that He wants me to do something to help Bo.

"So you looked up the verse?"

"Yes. And one Katherine sent me."

"Hmm."

She punched Crystal's arm again. "I'm not *that* fragile."

"Okay." Crystal jumped off the sofa before she could be assaulted again. "I'm gonna get a soda. You want anything?"

She shook her head and pressed the play button. The characters on the TV screen jumped into action.

~ * ~

Bo stared at the stained mattress and metal bars holding it. How had he ended up there? Juvi. The word clutched his heart and squeezed like a boa. He didn't like hanging out in his room at home. He didn't even care about sitting inside watching TV or playing video games like so many guys at school. No, he'd rather be outside on any given day. Even if a storm blew in, that only made him retreat to the barn or the porch to watch. And now he sat stuck in a six by ten cinderblock cell. It couldn't get any worse.

He groaned. Not only was he trapped indoors without the slightest ray of sunshine or drop of fresh air, but he also had murder charges hanging over his head. Murder charges.

He didn't like Stacy. Hated her, to be honest. That was no secret. But he never would've laid a hand on her.

According to the lawyer, the police had found a puncture in the brake line on Stacy's car. Since he'd been outside while she talked to Jeremy and they knew he despised her, they concluded he'd done the damage. Mr. Wiser had said Bo's best hope lay in the fact that the prosecutors had to prove he'd done it. Beyond a reasonable doubt.

The knots in his neck told him differently.

He threw himself off the bed and began pacing. He pulled every word the lawyer had said and studied them like he would a new horse. Getting to know it, feel it out, and learn how to approach it. He liked Mr. Wiser. Normally, he thought lawyers weren't worth the oxygen they used up, but this guy seemed all right. Genuine. He wanted to help Bo. Believed he didn't do the things the police accused him of.

Because of Dana.

The serpent around his heart tightened its grip. Dana. Did she believe him? Would she be willing to wait this stupid thing out?

Her parents had, after all, gotten him a lawyer. That still blew him away. He knew they didn't like him. Maybe they trusted Dana enough to support him because she did.

That had to mean she believed him.

At least he hadn't lost everything. He still had his family and

Dana.

And one day, maybe, he'd also have his freedom again.

A twinge in his heart caught him off guard. It felt different than the tightness that had taken hold the last two days. He stopped pacing and dropped down on the bed. At least his roommate had gone to the church service they held, leaving him to get some peace and quiet.

Church. Humph. Dana had probably gone to church that morning, too. He glared at the belly of the top bunk again as the twinge in his heart tugged tighter. He almost wished he could believe in the God Dana believed in. Almost.

~ * ~

Dana gazed out the window. She'd grabbed a burger and fries on the way to Bo's house after church. His mom hugged her and gushed over the lawyer. Mr. Singer thanked Dana, but mostly kept his lips tight, making it clear he thought she was intruding on their time with Bo by showing up to go with them. She held back a smirk. That's where Bo got his jaw-clenching, disapproving expression from. Being able to read his dad would definitely come in handy.

Silence filled the car. Dana suspected the weight of where they were going sat on them as the car wound its way through the three counties between home and Bo. It sat on Dana, too.

The words from this morning's sermon pushed their way through.

'Trust in the Lord with all your heart and lean not on your own understanding; in all your ways submit to him and he will make your paths straight.'

Proverbs 3:5-6. Those were verses she knew, but wouldn't necessarily have applied to her current situation. But they fit. And they went along with the verses on faith she'd looked up the night before. She needed to trust God, to lean on Him. Follow His guidance and He'd show her what to do.

She'd almost fallen out of the pew when Pastor John talked about God moving the boulders in the path of life in Sunday school. Again with the obstacles and letting God take care of them. Mountains, boulders, obstacles. God would take care of them all. And show her what she needed to do.

Her throat tightened as the road and grass flew by. Could she really do anything to help Bo?

She swallowed it down and blinked back tears. She could do something. She would do something. She simply had to wait on God to show her what it would be.

Chapter 21

The door clicked shut behind Dana, Bo's parents, and their escort. She emptied her pockets, leaving her cell phone in a locker. She signed in, writing her name and time of arrival below the Singers' names. A buzzer sounded and they walked through a steel door with a tiny window. The door behind them clicked to signal its relocking. Precious seconds ticked away before a second buzzer sounded and the opposite door opened.

Goose bumps covered Dana's arms as they entered the open, stark white room. It held nothing but a few tables, chairs, a couple other families, and three guards. Glassed doors broke up the room's solid, concrete walls. One of them led to what looked like a cafeteria and others held classrooms. Two solid doors labeled as bathrooms framed a water fountain. A door like the ones they'd come through opened and Bo followed a guard through it. He wore blue pants and matching shirt and held his hands behind his back. She shivered. That must be where the cells were.

She fixed her eyes on Bo as he took a seat and talked with his parents. His mom updated him on the horses and Jeremy's progress. The way Mrs. Singer talked somebody would think she hadn't seen Bo in a year, instead twenty-four hours.

Dana understood. It seemed like forever since she'd seen him at school two days before. So much had changed in that short time. So many things, except her feelings for him. Those wouldn't change. She'd love him 'til the day she died.

He met her gaze and his hand scooted across the table to cover hers. His mom kept babbling about the farm.

I love you, Dana mouthed.

He winked and a smirk crept onto his lips.

Mrs. Singer took a break and glanced at Dana and Bo's touching hands. She stood and excused herself to go to the restroom. Mr. Singer mumbled something about stretching his legs.

Bo leaned forward and squeezed her hand. "You came."

"Of course I came." She wove her fingers between his. "I couldn't stand the thought of you being locked up here. Not getting to see you or talk to you."

He rubbed the back of her hand with his thumb.

"Jeremy told me about the lawyer."

His eyebrows shot up. "Jeremy told you? You mean your parents didn't?"

"No." She chuckled. "They didn't tell me a thing. I asked them about it and my dad said, 'Well, a boy can't go to jail because he has an incompetent lawyer.' My mom shrugged it off, said it wasn't a big deal."

"It's a big deal." His gaze held hers.

"I know." Dana swallowed hard. "Jeremy said you have a hearing tomorrow."

"Yeah. Something about them giving the evidence to the judge. Then he decides whether it goes through and whether I get to go home now or not."

"It sure would be nice if you could come home tomorrow."

"You're telling me. But Mr. Wiser said not to expect it. They'll keep me in this cage until the trial."

"That'll be in three weeks, right?"

"Most likely. Unless they ask for a continuance, saying they're not ready. But Mr. Wiser's gonna push for it to go through quickly. There's not really any evidence to gather anyway." His head hung low and his shoulders shook with a sigh.

Dana pulled his hand to her lips and kissed the back of each of his fingers. "So what happens in the meantime?"

"Nothing. I sit here and we wait."

"What about proving you're innocent."

"There's nothing to prove. On our end, anyway. They have

to try to prove I did it. We have to make the judge doubt I did."

"There's nothing else?"

His shoulders sunk further. "Nope."

She hated this. She wanted to pound the table. Knock some sense into these people. They were crazy thinking he could have done such a thing. If only they could see what being here was doing to him. Of course, they probably wouldn't care.

Oh, Lord, help me to trust in You. I know there's something I can do, I just don't know what yet. Show me what it is. And show Bo that You're in control.

"Dana?"

"Yeah?"

"What was that all about?"

Heat rose to her cheeks. He couldn't know she'd been praying. And she wasn't about to offer the information. "Nothing. Thinking and wishing I could do something about you being here."

"Okay. if you're sure. You had a funny look on your face."

Dana shrugged. The Singer's walked from the other side of the room towards the table with a guard. Their time must be up.

She kissed the tip of his left ring finger. "I love you. Don't forget that. No matter what. And I'll try to write you. They said I could."

"Okay. I love you, too."

She grinned. "And if I use text lingo in my letters, you'll understand, right?"

One side of his mouth turned up. "Right."

"Bo, we'll come back Wednesday. That's the next visitation day." Mr. Singer looked at Dana, then back at his son. "I'm sure Jeremy will want to come with us, too."

Her heart sank. That meant she wouldn't be able to come again until next weekend. A whole week without seeing him.

At least that'd give her plenty of free time to work on clearing his name.

Dana retrieved her phone on their way out of the detention center and saw a text waiting from Katherine. *"Don't forget we're helping w/ Vacation Bible School this week. B @ church by 8:45 2morrow."*

She held back a groan. Part of her wanted to spend every waking moment figuring out how to help Bo. The other part of her looked forward to having something to take her mind off everything. Especially since she had no clue where to start.

~ * ~

Monday morning, Dana met Katherine at church and they helped with crafts for the younger kids. For almost three straight hours every morning that week she glued, glittered, and glossed her time away. Her mom greeted her every day with lunch and a new project when she got home. Dana's mom had randomly decided to plant a garden this year and had Dana help her can tomatoes, green beans, and other 'freshly picked' things. Her mom thought she was doing her a favor by keeping her busy, but she didn't know Dana needed time to figure out how to help Bo. She bubbled over with excitement about her garden and making things they could eat all year long, so Dana kept her teeth clamped tightly on her tongue when she wanted to scream.

Her plans to spend her afternoons researching ways to help Bo before heading back to church for youth VBS disappeared like a tumbleweed across the prairie. Friday night came quicker than a mid-afternoon thunderstorm.

Dana plunked into her desk chair. A whole week gone, and she still hadn't done anything to help Bo. Her eyes drooped, but she hadn't written her daily letter to him yet.

Her pen flew over the paper. After finishing the two and a half pages, she checked it over. She'd told him how much she loved him. How much she believed in him. How she couldn't wait to see him again. Everything was there. Everything except the time she'd spent at church.

"God, I'd love to tell Bo about helping out at church this week, but I just can't risk hurting him more right now. I trust you'll work on his heart and one day I'll be able to share church with him, too."

She sprayed a dash of perfume on the envelope and left it on her desk to mail the next morning. Just like she'd done every night that week.

Crawling into bed, she pulled her covers up and welcomed sleep.

~*~

The letter she'd composed the night before lay fresh in Dana's hands. She'd see him in a few hours, but she'd still mail the letter. Then he'd get it next week on a day she couldn't be there. And he'd know. Nothing had changed.

But everything felt different. Her days were no longer filled with horses and hay and her guy. They were full of laughing children, relay games, and Bible stories. Bo would have been furious had he been home that week. She bit the inside of her mouth. Her heart longed for him to come home. The thought of losing her time at church, losing her new friends, losing the support she had there tied her stomach in knots. There had to be a way two things she cared about most would work together, but she couldn't figure out how.

Her Bible caught her eye and she ran her fingers across it. *I know. Have faith in You to work it out. I just don't see how it will.*

Dana whipped her hair into a ponytail, licked the flap on the envelope, and sealed it. The knots in her stomach taunted her as she walked across the room. There had to be something for her to do to help his case.

She spritzed the perfume on her neck and wrists and headed down the hallway. Would he still want to be with her when he came home and found out about the church thing?

The sun blasted her as she pushed open the front door, letter clutched in her left hand.

God, give me something.

She opened the mailbox, inserted the letter, closed the door, and raised the flag. Turning to walk back down her driveway to the house, a clanking caught her attention. She twisted her neck to see an El Camino cruising down her street. Old Tom's old car. He refused to get rid of that thing, claiming it was perfect: half car, half truck. Even though it had regular visits to the repair shop.

The shop. She spun and fled to the road, waving Old Tom down. He slowed to a stop and stuck his thinning, grey-topped head out the window. "Hey, Dana."

She shielded the sun from her eyes with her hand. "Hey, Tom. How's the old car doing?"

"Got a rattle, but still a kickin'." He reached out and patted the door like Bo would a horse that had ridden well.

Dana grinned. "I see. Hey, do you have a shop that's really good? That has someone who's like an expert on cars?"

His head bobbed. "Yep. Sure do. Mac's place on the other side of town. Chip Watkins is their top mechanic and the best in town. Your car givin' ya trouble?"

"Um." She cleared her throat. "Not exactly. I just want to talk to someone about a car question I have."

"Well, Chip's your guy."

"Okay, thanks."

"Absolutely. Catch ya later."

She headed towards the house wearing a grin. A mechanic. A car expert. That's who could help her out. She had to find out more about that punctured brake line. It was the key to the cause of the accident.

As she reached for the doorknob, a groan escaped. She smacked herself on the forehead. Chip *Watkins*. He had to be related to Chet. All the Watkins in the tiny town were related.

Her hopes at asking Old Tom for another recommendation rattled down the street and disappeared. She sighed and turned the knob. She'd have to take her chances. Even the threat of running into Chet wouldn't stop her from helping to clear Bo's name.

She grabbed the phone book from the magazine rack next to the sofa and flipped through the pages until she found 'Mac's Mechanics.' She typed the number into her phone and hit save. The screen glared the time at her. Eleven-thirty. No chance to go by there before meeting Bo's parents. They'd be closed by the time she got home. And they wouldn't be open the next day. It'd have to wait two more days. Two more days closer to Bo's trial.

Chapter 22

Bo watched Dana and his parents walk away as a guard escorted them out through one of the dozens of metal doors keeping him locked away from his life. He stood and clasped his hands behind his back, then silently followed another guard through the now-familiar series of doors to his cell. They called them rooms. Humph. Their standards for what they called a room were lower than low.

The door clicked shut behind him. His roommate lay on the top bunk. Lou's almost-bald head was propped up on a couple of sorry excuses for pillows. Reading. Bo shook his head. He never could understand how somebody could lay around reading for hours on end.

"Have a good visit?"

Bo looked up. "Yeah."

Lou set his book down and rolled to his side. "Your folks again?"

"Yeah. And Dana."

His roommate grinned. "The girlfriend."

Bo smirked. "Yeah."

"Is that all you can say? 'Yeah.'"

His smirk widened. "No."

"Funny guy. Too bad they don't have visitation every day.

You don't quite look like a horse needing to be shot today."

"Visitation's good. But there's still the other twenty-three hours of being hog-tied in this place." Bo plunked down on his bed and looked up at Lou's face leaning over the edge of the top bunk. "What about you? I haven't seen you go out for visitation. Where's your family?"

Lou's brow furrowed, then relaxed. "I don't have one."

"How can you not have a family?"

Lou's eyes clouded. "My dad was never around. My mom refused to say anything about him. The one time I asked her when I was five she answered with the back of her hand. On my seventh birthday she celebrated by having some friends over. *Her* friends. They brought a keg and some coke and got too loud. The police showed up and carted everybody away. They didn't know I was hiding under my bed."

Bo whistled. "Man. That's rough."

"Yeah. I got hungry a couple days later when I ran out of cereal and crackers. I wondered next door to ask for something to eat and they called social services."

"So, you're a foster kid."

Lou scoffed. "A foster kid. Whatever that means. A kid without a home. Until now."

"Now?" Bo gestured to the tiny cinder block space. "This is no home."

Lou's face relaxed, his eyes shone, and he smiled. He pulled the brown book with the map on the cover and tapped his finger on it. "Here. I found my home here."

He sat up and read the cover. "Archeological Study Bible." He rolled his eyes and laid back down. Of course a guy without family would turn to some made-up stories about a God.

Dana had a family and believed in that same God.

He shook the thought aside. "That may do it for you. But I have a family. I don't need a crutch."

Lou chuckled. "It's not a crutch. It's a life-saver. I got myself into this place and can't get out. But now that doesn't matter. I'm free in here." He tapped his chest. "And it's a freedom no one can take away from me."

"Okay. Soon I'll really be free. I'll be back on the farm with my family and with Dana. That's all I need."

"And if you don't get out?"

Bo blanched at the thought. He hadn't done anything. Of course he'd get out. But that nagging knot in his stomach tightened. Even the lawyer didn't seem totally sure about his future.

He had to get out. Or else he'd go crazy. "I will." His voice echoed more confidence than he felt.

"I hope so, man." Lou disappeared as he rolled onto his back. "I'll be prayin' for you."

He closed his eyes. He wished people would stop saying that. Prayers weren't what he needed. He needed something to happen. Something to get him out of this mess.

~ * ~

Dana stared at the screen on her laptop, the sixth or seventh website she'd been to investigating how brake lines worked and how they got punctured. So far she'd learned more about cars than she'd ever wanted to know, but came up as empty as a pig wrestler covered in grease.

Her phone rang and Katherine's info popped up.

"Hello?"

"Hey. What are you doing tomorrow?"

"Going to church, then…nothing. Watching a movie maybe."

"Why don't you go to a concert with me? Anna was supposed to go, but she's been throwing up all day."

"I guess I could do that." Dana scanned the screen. "I don't have anything better to do. Where is it?"

"In Houston at five, so we'll have to leave right after church. My aunt lives there and we can spend the night with her afterwards."

"Houston! You think my parents are going to let me drive to Houston for a concert?"

"Come on. Ask 'em. It's a Christian concert. They can talk to my parents and my aunt and everything. You'll love it. It'll be great."

"A Christian concert, huh? They might, I don't know. Who is it?"

"G-note. I'm sure they'll let you go. Didn't you say your mom's been driving you crazy trying to distract you from thinking about Bo?"

"Yeah." Going would mean getting home late Monday. Maybe she'd have time to go by Mac's before they closed. "I'll ask. I think they'll be home after dinner."

"Call 'em and see."

"Okay, I will. I'll text you what they say."

"Great."

"Oh, hey. G-note. I've never heard of them."

Katherine's laughter filled the line. "It's a him. He has a backup band, but, well, anyway, you'll like it, I promise."

"If you say so." She hung up and dialed her mom's cell.

"Hello?"

"Hey, Mom. It's me."

"Hi, Sweetie. How'd it go today?"

"Fine. It was good to see Bo."

"I'm sure it was. Did he have any news from Mr. Wiser?"

"No, nothing new. His court date is definitely two weeks from Monday."

"Well, I'm sure they'll come up with something, dear."

Dana hoped so. She stuck her free hand in her back pocket. "Mom, Katherine called and she has an extra ticket to a Christian concert in Houston tomorrow and wants me to go."

"Houston?"

"We'd have to leave right after church and stay with her aunt afterwards."

"I don't know, honey. That's an awful long way to drive for a concert."

Dana rolled her eyes. "It's only three hours, Mom. We'll be careful and I'll call to check in a million times. You can call Katherine's mom and talk to her. I'll give you her number."

"Yes. Let me talk to her mother and then I'll call you back with an answer."

Dana gave her mom the number and hung up. She stared at the computer screen and clicked back to her search results page. She skimmed over the page, making it about half-way down when her phone rang. Her mom's picture popped up on the screen.

"Well?"

"You can go."

She closed the windows and stood. "Thanks." She strolled over to her closet.

"I expect a call when you get there and when the concert's

over. And when you leave to come home Monday."

"Okay. I got it. Call every half hour." She had no idea what to wear to a Christian concert.

"All right smarty britches. Just be glad I'm letting you go."

She pulled out a turquoise blouse and held it up. Nope, too short. "Yes, Ma'am."

"That's better. I'll be home before you go to bed. Are you going to ride to church with us in the morning?"

"Umm, I don't know. That might work. Then I can leave with Katherine. I'll double check."

"Okay. Don't forget to pack your toothbrush and phone charger."

How old was she? Two? Dana pulled a red tank top out of the closet. Bo's favorite.

"Mom, I'm seventeen. I won't forget."

The tank top's V-neck didn't cut very low, but fit tighter than she should wear. She ran her fingers through her hair. She'd been wearing it the night Jeremy'd had the accident. It had only been a couple months ago, but felt like years at times.

She hung the red tank top back up and grabbed a hot pink t-shirt. That should work.

Her mom's voice still rattled in her ear. "So I'll see you in a few hours."

"Okay."

She found a pair of not-to-short shorts, grabbed other necessary items and began stuffing them in her overnight bag. She caught a glimpse of herself in the mirror as she packed her extra toothbrush and toothpaste. The face staring back at her looked almost happy. It was nice to have something fun to look forward to. She grinned.

And she'd be home in time to go to Mac's before they closed Monday.

Chapter 23

People of all shapes, sizes, colors, hair styles, and clothing surrounded Dana. Some even had tattoos and lip piercings. She clamped her mouth shut so her jaw wouldn't fall to the ground. It was not what she thought a Christian concert would be like. People whooped and hollered, jumped and swayed, threw their hands in the air and yelled an occasional 'Amen.'

The beat of the music reminded her of what she listened to before moving to Texas. The rhythm triggered something familiar deep inside and she found herself unable to stay in her seat. The words, though, the words were the complete opposite of the self-centered, arrogant, crude words of the music she used to listen to. Instead, these songs praised God. They sang about dedicating one's whole life, giving up everything, for God.

She closed her eyes and let the words rain down and quench her soul. She raised her hands to the God who hadn't given up on her when she'd given up on Him. A lump rose in her throat and gratefulness moistened her eyes.

The music died down and she opened her eyes.

"How ya doing tonight, Houston?" G-note asked. The crowd went wild.

He kept talking, gripping Dana with every word.

"Now, I'd like to talk to all the single ladies with us

tonight." Screams swelled. "Remember, that boy who wants to step to you, make sure he loves God with all his heart, mind, and soul. He can't love you right 'til he loves your Lord."

The crowd cheered while the lump in Dana's throat that had been gratitude suddenly sank to the pit of her stomach. The words volleyed in her head. *He can't love you right 'til he loves your Lord.*

Dana clasped her throat with her hand. *I can't stay with Bo if he doesn't love God.* She knew it as sure as she knew the wind was what whipped her hair around her face. It couldn't be seen, but it was as real and true as anything. She stood stock still until a hand touched her arm.

Katherine leaned towards her. "Are you okay?"

Wide-eyed, Dana shook her head.

"Bo?"

She nodded.

Katherine's hand slid down to hers and squeezed it. "It'll be okay."

A tear slid down her cheek. The plum-sized lump had made its way back up and kept her from uttering a sound.

Katherine's arm slipped around her. "It'll be okay. I promise."

How? How would it be all right?

Bo sat in jail accused of murder. She'd vowed to help him, to never stop loving him.

God had drawn Dana back to Himself and became her utmost priority. That would leave room for Bo only if he shared her faith. He didn't.

She struggled to breathe. She couldn't give up Bo. But she had to.

Katherine sang along with the band and crowd, but didn't release her grip on Dana. Tears streamed down Dana's face. Lyrics, shouts, and bodies blurred.

"I'm all yours." The first words she'd heard since those last, devastating words. That's what she used to tell Bo.

I'm yours and always will be. She'd tell it to him while stroking her thumb on the back of his hand or running her fingers through his thick, sandy-blond hair.

I like it that way and plan to keep it that way forever, he'd whisper in her ear before covering her mouth with his.

"I'm all yours, Lord," the song continued. This song, like

too many of the others, seemed to talk directly to her and slice into her heart. No way it could be a coincidence

She should be God's. Totally. Not divided between God and Bo.

The blade in her heart twisted. The pain radiated, building a scream from deep within. She swallowed, refusing to let it release.

Katherine continued to sway and sing. Dana squeezed her eyes closed, forcing the tears to stop. Katherine's arm tightened around her.

She had to get out of there. She glanced at her friend. There had to be something she could come up with as an excuse to leave.

Her mental search found nothing and her lack of a decision kept her glued to her spot. She swallowed hard.

God, give me strength. I can't do this.

Slowly, the rhythms around her made their way through. The words began to click in her mind. Like a jumbled mess of cords being unwound one by one, the muddled sounds became clear.

"…I'll give up everything for a glimpse of You…" The song rang out.

That's exactly the opposite of what she'd done. She'd given up on God, the owner of her soul, for the everything else in her life. Bo had become her world.

Oh, God, forgive me. And help me. Help Bo. He has to come to you. He has to. But if he doesn't, help me be strong enough to walk away.

Dana raised both hands and gave everything to God. She stood there. Heart breaking. Soul listening. Mind battling.

She had no idea how she'd ever give up Bo. But she couldn't give up God again. How those two things would come together she couldn't imagine.

It all seemed impossible.

~ * ~

"You've been awfully quiet." Katherine pulled Dana from her tortured stare out the passenger side window.

"Just thinking."

"About Bo?"

"Yeah."

Katherine paused. When Dana didn't elaborate, she pressed on. "Anything specific?"

She dropped her head back on the headrest. "He doesn't believe in God."

"I know," Katherine whispered.

"I can't stay with him if he doesn't share my faith."

Katherine sighed. "So what does that mean?"

"I don't know. I can't leave him now. That's beyond cruel. Not only do I not want to leave him, but I promised myself I'd do everything I could to help him. I even felt like God wants me to help him."

"How?" Katherine steered the car into the left lane to pass a pokey farm truck.

"I plan on going to see a mechanic this afternoon. To find out more about what could have caused the cut in Stacy's brake line. I know Bo didn't do it, so how'd it happen? That's what I want to find out."

"Wouldn't the police have looked into that?"

Dana scoffed. "They didn't look into anything. They found out the brake line had a leak and that Bo didn't like Stacy and they assumed the worst."

"Hmm." Katherine switched back to the right lane.

"Does God want me to break up with Bo now and desert him at the worst time of his life? Or stay with him and help him through this? And then how do I go, 'I love you and I'm glad you're out of jail, but can't be with you.'?"

Her words hung in the air as they sped down the empty, flat road.

"I thought I'd have all the answers when I turned my life back over to God. Now it seems more complicated than ever."

"God doesn't promise easy. He just promises to show you what to do and not to leave you."

"So why isn't He making it clear what I should do?" She turned towards her friend.

"He will." Katherine glanced her way. "Have you been praying about it?"

"Only all the time."

"Are you listening? Or just talking?"

The answer came weakly. "Talking."

"Start listening. He'll show you what to do."

Dana leaned back and closed her eyes. Start listening. So how would she quiet the chaos in her head and do that?

Chapter 24

Dana's mom flung the door open like she'd been waiting for Dana all morning. "How was the concert?"

"Great." She dropped her bag and sank into the recliner. "Not at all what I expected."

"How so?"

"Oh, I don't know. Just…well, everyone wasn't cookie cutter, goody-two-shoes looking. And it was actually really good music."

Her mom grinned. "Not boring ole' churchy music?"

She smiled. "No."

"And what about where you stayed?"

"Katherine's aunt has a cute little house. She kept us up all night." She yawned. "She'd just gotten back from a mission trip to Peru last week and told us all about it."

"A mission trip, huh?"

"Yeah." Dana yawned again. "I'd love to tell you more about it, but I wanta go unpack. And maybe find some caffeine."

"All right. I'll look forward to hearing more later." Her mom checked her watch. " There's a retirement party for one of the nurses at the hospital. I'm leaving in a few minutes. Dinner tonight maybe?"

She headed back through the den with a can of soda and grabbed her bag. "Sure. That'll work."

In her room, she tossed her bag by the door, popped open the soda, and crashed onto her bed. Leaning against the mound of pillows, she took the first sip, letting the fizz tickle her throat and waiting for the caffeine to take effect.

Start listening.

Okay, God. Here I am. I'm listening. What do I do?

She sat quietly and downed the entire twelve ounces of energy. She didn't hear anything, nor did the magic elixir help keep her droopy eyes propped open. Setting the empty can on her bedside table, she rolled over and buried her head in her pillow. She dozed, but woke several times. When she did, she prayed again for direction. Her phone buzzed in the middle of her prayer and she glanced at the alarm clock beside her bed. Seven-thirty. She grabbed her phone and read Crystal's message.

"How was the concert? Guess what. Max met w/pastor 2day & going 2 b baptized! How cool. Mayb u can come to my church that Sun."

She fell back onto the fluffy hill. Would she ever be able to share the same thing about Bo?

Dana clicked off her reply. *"That's great. Let me know when."*

It seemed so easy for Crystal. Max turned around and started going to church as soon as they'd begun dating. Maybe if she'd still been going to church when she and Bo met….

No. He probably wouldn't have ever asked her out. But now that he loved her, maybe there was something she could do to change his mind, make him open up and at least consider it.

"Thx. Praying 4 u."

Pray.

She could pray for him. She had been, but she could keep on.

And she could love him.

She pulled her knees to her chest and hugged them. She couldn't go see Bo again. Not until all this was over. Sitting across from him and pretending nothing had changed would be impossible.

She closed her eyes. If she couldn't go see him, maybe she could still write. Still work to clear his name.

Dana listened.

No, she couldn't write him every day as if nothing had changed. She couldn't pretend to pour out her heart in ink when she'd be holding back the most important thing to her.

And yes. She'd work every spare moment she had to prove his innocence.

Getting up, she strolled to her desk and pulled out her personalized notebook paper and pen from her bedside drawer. She took a deep breath and began writing.

Bo,

Sorry I didn't get a letter to you yesterday. Katherine and I went to a concert in Houston and stayed with her aunt. It was amazing, but you wouldn't have liked it. It wasn't country.

I won't be able to come see you next weekend. I can't explain now. I won't be able to write, either. Don't think I don't love you. My heart aches for you more than ever. I love you. I love you. I love you. Don't ever forget that. I know you're innocent and can't wait to see you out of there.

You never leave my thoughts.

My love always,
Dana

She read and reread the letter. There was so much she left out. Couldn't write. She couldn't tell him that the concert had been a Christian one and touched her in ways she had no words to explain. She wanted to go into the tiniest detail of why she wouldn't visit him again. But how to make him understand? He'd probably become even more angry with God.

She hoped Bo would believe she still loved him. She did. Even if that wouldn't change the decision she'd made to cut him out of her life. He didn't know that, though. Didn't need to right now.

Maybe he'd believe her love. Feel her love. Know that she continued to fight for him.

Folding the letter, she kissed it, and slipped it into an envelope. She sealed it, stamped it, and left it sitting on her desk. Forcing back the tears that threatened to erupt, she picked up her Bible and desperately sought some kind of peace about letting go of the man she loved more than anyone else on the earth.

~ * ~

Dana drove down her driveway the next morning and slipped the letter in her mailbox. She pulled away quickly so she wouldn't grab the envelope and its contents back out and rip them to shreds.

At the end of her street, she sat at the stop sign an extra few breaths and checked her GPS. It showed that she'd be at Mac's shop in twenty-one minutes. Questions about Bo's reaction to the letter mixed with ones she wanted to ask Chip. She patted the spiral notebook on the seat next to her. Good thing she'd scribbled her questions down. She didn't trust herself to remember everything. She tucked a lock of hair behind her ear, bit her lip, and turned left on Maple Street.

Gravel crunched under her tires as she parked beside the ancient-looking garage. Cars with dents, missing parts, and faded paint littered the parking lot and grass beyond. Five bay doors lined the far side of the building, with a smaller, glassed area standing closest to where she parked. She took a deep breath and stepped out of the car.

Clutching her notebook in one hand and pen in the other, she entered through the door with an 'open' sign hanging from the inside. A bell jingled her arrival and the smells of gas, oil, and paint assaulted her. A guy with shaggy, blond hair walked through an open door to her left.

He wiped his greasy hands on a stained rag. "Can I help you?"

She cleared her throat. "I'd like to see Chip Watkins."

"You on the schedule?"

"No." She twirled her pen between her fingers. "I wanted to ask him some questions."

"You got car issues?"

"Not exactly."

Mr. Full-of-Questions cocked his head to the side and raised an eyebrow. "I'll get 'im."

"Thanks," Dana mumbled. She leaned against the counter, tapped her pen, and glanced at the clock on the wall. Her nerves increased with every tick of the second hand.

An older version of Chet walked through the door and she swallowed the bile that rose in her throat.

"I'm Chip." He even sounded like Chet. Voice maybe a tad bit deeper.

"Hi, I'm Dana. I wondered if I could ask you some questions." She clicked her pen open and poised it over her notebook.

He pressed a tab on a hand-washing bottle hanging on the door and rubbed the gritty solution on his hands. He pulled a rag from his back pocket to dry them as his gaze traveled from her head to her toes and back again. "Questions, huh?"

She bit her tongue and composed herself. *Just get what you need.* "Yes. About a busted brake line."

Chip squinted. "Brake line…" He stuck the rag back in his pocket. "Dana…Dana…" His eyes widened. "You're Bo Singer's girlfriend. He cut Stacy Athen's brake line."

Don't bite. Ignore everything he says except about the car. She needed his help. She gritted her teeth and willed her aggravation not to show itself. "He did not cut Stacy's brake line and that's what I'm here about. I want to know what else could have caused it."

"You say he didn't do it." He looked at the clock. "And you want me to help you. I'm a busy guy. Lots of cars out there to fix. Who says I have time to talk guesses about accidents."

What an arrogant, self-centered oaf.

Might as well play into that.

She relaxed her jaw, tightened her ponytail, and forced a smile. "Look, I heard you were the best. The one to come to with any car questions."

He leaned against the door frame. "Well, that's true."

"So, have you ever seen a brake line get damaged any other way?" She touched the tip of the pen to the notebook.

"Yeah. Once in a while. If a car's old, the brake line's rusty, and hits something sharp, it can get punctured."

"Old like eight years?"

"I guess. If it was a cheap car."

Dana scribbled. "So what kind of something sharp could do that?"

He scratched his head. "I don't know. A big stick, I guess. A rock. Not a small one, but a big 'un."

"Okay, anything else?"

"Anything laying in the road that came up high enough and was hard enough."

She flipped the page.

"So how long would it take to leak out?"

"Huh?"

"The fluid. How long would it be before the brakes failed?"

"That depends on a few things. How fast the car was going. If the fluid was low. How big the gash was. Things like that."

"Let's say the car was on a long dirt lane, like a mile long and the car drove slow, like five or ten miles an hour."

"I s'pose."

"Great." She flipped to the next page. "And would the brake fluid that leaked out be easy to spot?"

"Yeah, should be. Especially if the gash was big enough."

Dana tapped her pen on the counter. It hadn't rained in weeks. Dust might have covered the fluid, but some should still be there. "One more question." Her smile widened.

"Sure, Babe. I got time for one more." His gaze grazed her again.

Keeping her eyes from rolling, she glanced at the last question on her notebook. "Is there any way a small leak could take a long time to cause brakes to go out? Like more than half an hour?" Dana had calculated the time it took Stacy to get down their driveway, talk to Jeremy, and leave at least a dozen times. Thirty minutes was the minimum time it could have taken. She had to know if, by some random chance, Stacy's line could have been punctured before she got to the Singer's house.

"Not unless it was a pinhole."

She closed her notebook and clicked her pen shut. "Thanks. That's all I needed."

"You sure that's all you needed?" said a deep voice from behind her.

Dana spun around. How had she missed the bell over the door ringing? She slipped her pen into the spiral of her notebook. "Yes, Chet, I'm sure." She turned back to Chip. "Thanks again."

He grinned. "No problem. You come back any time."

She turned to leave and grimaced. Chet filled the doorway. "What's the hurry, Dana? There's no boyfriend to go run and see. That is, unless today's visitation day at juvi."

"Only in a hurry to leave since you arrived."

He scrunched up his face. "Ouch. No need to be mean. I just thought I'd offer to take you to lunch since Bo's unavailable."

"There's no other way to get through to you. I'm not interested. Even if Bo weren't in the picture, I wouldn't be interested. You may think you're God's gift to every female in town, but it's a gift I'll pass on."

"We'll see." He stepped closer. "When that boyfriend of yours finds himself locked up for twenty years you'll realize what you're missing." His voice lowered. "I can do things for you Bo would never think of, treat you like you deserve." Chet ran two fingers down her arm.

She shivered. "When it snows in Texas on July fourth, then I might think about considering your offer." She stepped around him and pushed the door open. "But I doubt it."

The door slammed behind her and she didn't look back until she'd gotten a couple miles down the road. Chet hadn't followed her. Not that he had any reason to. No reason other than he seemed to push harder the more she said no. Another shiver travelled up her spine. She couldn't for the life of her figure out what other girls saw in that creep.

She shook the grime of running into Chet off and rested her hand on her notebook. She had gotten what she went for. Best case scenario Stacy's car could have been leaking fluid for a long time. From what Chip had said, that wasn't likely. But something else could have caused the gash as she left the Singer's house. Their driveway had plenty of bumps, rocks, roots, and sticks. The trees on either side constantly dropped dead limbs.

Her heart told her to drive straight to Bo's house and go over the driveway like a rancher inspecting a horse, noting each and every detail. What would it be like to be there knowing she'd shoved Bo away in the letter she sent this morning? She wasn't sure she could face Jeremy or his parents if she ran into them. They'd want to know why she'd come over and she had no clue what she'd say.

Dana ripped the rubber band out of her hair and let it flow around her shoulders. Was her headache from the ponytail, running into Chet, or pain traveling from her heart?

A few minutes later, she pulled into her own driveway and sat staring at the house, trying to figure out what to do next. This time listening worked. She got an answer.

Call the lawyer.

On the third ring, his voicemail picked up. "Mr. Wiser, this is Dana Little. Bo's girlfriend. I wanted to talk to you about something I think will help Bo. I talked to a mechanic today and he said almost anything could have punctured Stacy's brake line. Like a rock or big stick, or something. He also said there should be brake fluid from where it leaked. Thought it should be looked into. Thanks."

She ended the call and rested her head on the steering wheel. *God, is that all I can do? I know Bo is innocent. Show me how I can prove it.*

She had to prove it. Then she'd have to break Bo's heart.

Chapter 25

Dana stepped out of the shower with her towel wrapped around her. She checked her phone. He hadn't called yet. She yanked the brush through her hair. Mr. Wiser was a busy lawyer, she got that. But he seemed to care about Bo's case. Why wouldn't he return her call? It had been almost a whole day.

She tossed her brush in the drawer and got out her lotion. Working it into her face and arms, she went over the message she'd left him. No, she'd said enough. He should be right on it, calling her back.

She rubbed the lotion on her legs. Maybe he'd done something with the information and didn't want to contact her until he knew something more.

What would he do with it, though? She didn't know if he'd be able to look at the gash in Stacy's brake line. Or maybe he had the paperwork that gave him all the details. Maybe he didn't have time to follow up. Bo's trial was only a week and a half away.

She buttoned her shorts and slipped into a tank top. She pulled out her makeup bag. What if he didn't have time? He was a good lawyer, but had other clients.

Doubt swelled and she forced it back. She stared in the mirror at the light reflecting off light, medium, and dark blond hues in her hair. She closed her eyes.

I'm trying to listen, God. She covered her face with her hands and dropped to her knees.

Okay, I'm listening. Let Mr. Wiser listen, too, please. And show me what to do next.

Her phone sang. She pulled it out of her back pocket. "Hello?"

"Hey, girl. What cha doin'?"

"Hey, Crystal. Nothing. Just got out of the shower."

"You going somewhere today?"

She stood. "No. Don't have any plans."

"Good. I'll be there to pick you up in half an hour."

"Wait. What for?"

"You'll see. I have somewhere special to take you. It'll keep your mind off things."

She strolled to her bedroom and pulled her favorite flip flops out of her closet. She slipped them on. "What if I don't want my mind off things? What if I want to sit around and sulk?"

"Exactly. Come with me. It'll be…fun."

"You sure? You don't sound sure."

Crystal laughed. "Yeah. It'll be good."

Dana read the note her mom left on the kitchen counter. *Ran to the grocery store. French toast in the refrigerator. Love you, Mom.*

She opened the fridge and pulled out the waiting plate. "I don't know…"

"Yes, you do. I'll be there in twenty-five."

"But I-" The line went dead and she grinned. She planned to go the whole time, but had too much fun teasing Crystal to let her know that.

~ * ~

Dana added a message to the bottom of her mom's note. *Crystal kidnapped me. Call u later. L U 2*

She ran the brush through her hair once more and twisted it into a braid. She might as well get it out of the way. No telling what Crystal would get her into.

Waiting on the front steps, she ran her conversation with Chip through her mind. Did she forget to ask anything? She hoped not. She planned to never step foot in that place again. Chip might be the best mechanic around, but he leered at her the same way

Chet did. She shivered despite the already sweltering day. Sweat dripped down her back as her mind worked.

She stood when Crystal's car approached and met her in the driveway. Slamming the squeaky door behind her, she examined her best friend. "Okay. So where are we going?"

Crystal grinned. "Tyler."

"Tyler? What in the world for?" She cut her eyes at her friend. "You're not taking me shopping. You don't shop."

"No. Not shopping."

"You're not telling me, are you?"

"Nope." Her grin grew and her eyes twinkled.

That stubborn lock of hair already found its way out of her braid. She tucked it behind her ear. She didn't want to talk about Bo and hadn't told Crystal about not writing him. Not going to see him. Crystal would understand, but she'd picked Dana up to help get her mind off of Bo.

"Where's Max today?"

"Working."

"I should have known."

Crystal stuck her tongue out. "Smarty pants. I'd have still come and got you today."

She rolled her eyes. "Yeah, right."

"I would have." Crystal chuckled. "Max just would have come with us."

"Now I'm completely confused about where we're going."

"Good."

She tapped her fingers on the door handle. Her mind began to churn again. "So, how are things with Max?"

Crystal beamed and Dana didn't have to worry about making conversation for the rest of the almost hour drive.

~ * ~

'Eastern Mission,' the plain black and white sign sitting on an old concrete building read.

"This is where we're going?"

"Yep. The best way to not think about your problems is to help others with theirs."

Dana eyed the simple building. "What are we going to do?"

"I don't know. Wash sheets. Sort clothes. Help fix lunch.

Whatever they need?"

She crinkled her nose. "Wash sheets?"

"Yeah. It's a homeless shelter. They also collect and distribute donated clothes and serve breakfast and dinner." Crystal hopped out of the car. "I've got a couple bags of clothes in the trunk. Can you grab one?"

"Sure…"

She followed Crystal through the inconspicuous door lugging a black trash bag. Where'd she gotten them? Even Dana didn't have that many clothes to give away.

Standing inside the door, she let her eyes adjust from the bright sun to dim lights. The small room held several other bags of what she assumed were donated items. The buzz of people talking floated in from a door on the left. Above it a sign read, "The King will reply, 'Truly I tell you, whatever you did for one of the least of these brothers and sisters of mine, you did for me.' Matthew 25:40."

She dropped the bag next to the pile and glanced around. The room seemed clean, but cluttered.

"This way." Crystal led her to a short hallway which opened to a large dining room filled with old school tables. The kind with seats attached to them. A group of people sat at one of the tables. It looked like they were having a meeting.

A man who appeared about thirty, thin with crew cut hair, left the group and walked over to them. "Crystal, it's good to see you again. And you brought another friend."

Dana gaped at Crystal. She'd been there before?

"Dave, this is Dana."

"Hi, Dana. Nice to meet you. Thanks for coming out today."

"Sure." She slipped her hands into her back pockets.

"We're making the schedule for the next week." He motioned to the others hunched over some papers at the table. "We've got a lot to do. How long can y'all stay?"

Crystal eyed Dana. "I'm good all day. Through dinner?"

Through dinner? That was like eight hours. They hadn't even had lunch. She searched for an excuse to go home early, but came up empty. "Uh, sure."

"Great." Dave's smile showed perfectly straight teeth. "We had a church drop off some clothes they had left over from a yard sale and two of our regular volunteers have been sick this week.

Think you can start sorting them for us?"

"We'd love to. I brought a couple bags from my church, too."

"Fantastic. You know where everything goes?"

"Yep." Crystal looped her arm through Dana's. "Let's go."

Back in the cluttered room they first walked into, she pulled her arm free. "What else don't I know about you?"

Crystal grabbed a bag and lugged it across the room. She opened it and turned to Dana. "It's not a secret. You've been…busy lately."

Dana swallowed. *Guess I haven't been that great of a friend.* She checked her phone to make sure she hadn't missed the lawyers call and shoved it back in her pocket. "Okay. What do I do?"

Crystal flicked the light on. The room gave the impression as having once been an office. Counters on either side of the room, which probably served as desks at one time, were labeled with gender and size of clothes. Makeshift shelves had been added at shoulder height and bins with drawers poked out from underneath. The back wall held a bar that served as a hanging rack. "We go through those." Crystal pointed at the pile of bags. "Sort it and put it in here."

"All that's supposed to go in here?"

"Yeah. As much as possible."

Dana pulled a bag into what Dave had called a closet, sat on the floor, and began to pull things out. By the time she'd gotten to the bottom of the bag, she'd forgotten all about lunch.

~ * ~

Dana slumped into the passenger seat. "I'm whooped."

"Me, too. But did you think about Bo ?"

Her hand flew to her back pocket. She hadn't even checked for missed calls or messages since they began sorting the clothes. After working through the pile of bags, they helped serve dinner to a room full of smelly, dirty, friendly people. Her stomach had growled at the aroma of Swiss steak and garlic mashed potatoes, but they hadn't stopped to eat until after they'd served every last 'guest.'

"No. I didn't." She pulled her phone out. No calls. Three missed text messages. She zipped through them.

"You expecting a call?" Crystal pulled onto the main

highway.

"Hoping for one."

"From?"

Dana slipped her phone back in her pocket. "From Bo's lawyer. I called him with some information."

Crystal glanced at her with raised eyebrows and Dana spilled everything.

Chapter 26

Dana rolled over and groaned as the sunlight assaulted her. She checked her clock. Noon already.

After working at the shelter the day before, she'd been worn out, but her mom had rented a movie for them to watch. Not wanting to let her mom down after cancelling dinner, she'd stayed up instead of crawling immediately into bed.

Picking up her phone, she saw no missed calls. She flung her legs off the bed and got up.

Why hadn't the lawyer called her back? They were running out of time.

She dialed his number. Voicemail. She left another message.

Dana's phone vibrated as she stood at the sink rinsing her brunch dishes. Her heart leapt at seeing Mr. Wiser's name on the caller ID.

"Hello?"

"Is this Dana Little."

"Yes, it is."

"It's Ray Wiser. Sorry it took me so long to get back with you. I've been in court the last couple of days."

"Oh, that's okay." *Thank God you called.* "I wanted to talk to you about Bo's case."

"I gathered that from your message. There really isn't a

whole lot to do other than create doubt during the trial. We can't prove Bo didn't do it."

"I know. But if we can come up with some evidence, something to show it was just an accident, wouldn't that help?"

"It would. But I'm not sure what you're thinking."

"The mechanic I talked to said that something else could have caused the gash. A rock or big stick or something. The Singer's driveway is long and full of all sorts of stuff. Limbs from the trees fall on it all the time. I mean, couldn't she have hit something on the way?"

"I suppose…that would explain a lot." Silence filled the line.

"Did the police say anything about how big the gash was?"

"I have pictures, along with all the other evidence. It's part of discovery that they have to share. It's a decent gash." Papers rustled. "But…"

Hope filled Dana. "But what?"

"Well, I haven't gone over everything in detail yet because of this other case. I'm not sure. I've had my forensic guy look at it, and it doesn't look like a clean cut a knife would have made. Plus, the break line showed some age, which might have compromised its integrity."

"Okay." Her heart sped up. Had she actually found something helpful? "Also, the mechanic said the fluid would have started leaking right away. Did the police search for brake fluid? Do they know if it leaked where she'd parked, or started further down the driveway?"

More rustling papers. "I don't see anything here about brake fluid. It doesn't appear that they even looked for it. I'll review this today if I'm not called back into court for a verdict. I'll contact the investigating officer for the information."

"Thanks, Mr. Wiser. I know Bo's innocent. We just have to prove it."

"Thank you, Dana. You've asked questions I wouldn't have gotten around to until later this week. Bo sure is lucky to have you on his side."

Her eyes misted. "Yeah." She swallowed. "Can you call me when you hear something?"

Mr. Wiser chuckled. "I will let you know as soon as I know something."

She hung up. She was on Bo's side, but once she cleared his name and he returned home, she'd have to give him up. Probably forever.

~ * ~

Bo held the letter between his fingers. Mail time. The best time of the day. On days they didn't have visitation, anyway. And tomorrow would be visitation day again. The day Dana came with his parents.

Had it been only a week since he'd seen her?

Dana. His Dana. She'd knocked him off his feet the first time he saw her. He never imagined she'd say yes when he'd asked her out. But she did. And had been his ever since. No matter what her snotty cheerleader friends had said about him, she'd stuck by his side. Even now, with murder charges hanging over his head, she'd declared she didn't care what anyone else thought.

He held the envelope to his nose and sniffed. Hmm. No perfume. That wasn't like her. Maybe she forgot.

He slid his thumb under the flap to pop it open. Only one page. She usually wrote at least two, if not three or four.

He pulled the flimsy sheet out and unfolded it. His heart sped up as the words soaked in. He read them again. What did it mean? She swore she loved him. So why wasn't she coming to see him tomorrow? Why wouldn't there be any more letters? He read it again.

The concert. That had to have something to do with it. Or maybe she met somebody. He knew Chet was still after her. Now that Bo sat locked in a cage, he'd have free reign to reach Dana.

He read the gut-wrenching letter again.

Katherine. She went to Dana's church. Did that have something to do with it? He let the letter drop to the floor and balled his fists. He wanted to beat something. Wanted to hop on a horse and pound out his questions with the hooves clopping across endless fields. But he couldn't.

Lou's bald head poked around his mattress above Bo's head. "You all right?"

"Huh?"

"You grunted. Not the usual reaction you have to mail time."

"Yeah."

Lou scoped out the letter laying discarded on the floor. "Bad news?"

"I don't know."

"Okay. Wanna talk 'bout it?"

"No."

"All right." Lou's head disappeared.

Bo flung himself off the bed and paced. She loved him. She'd said so over and over. But she'd also said she couldn't come see him or write him. It made no sense.

He shook his head. Women.

He needed a blade of grass to chew. A horse to brush. Hay to gather. Something to do other than think and pace, pace and think.

Lou caught his eye.

"What?"

"Nothing." Lou returned his gaze to the familiar book that lay on his lap.

"How can you do that?"

"What?"

Bo waved his hand. "Read all the time. Especially that ancient, useless book."

Lou's eyes twinkled and he set the Bible aside. "I used to think that, too. Some of my foster families hauled me to church and prayed all the time. But then I'd be moved again and the beatings I got at some of the other houses blocked out the good memories. Those churchy houses were nice, but God obviously didn't care about me or he wouldn't have sent me to the bad houses."

Bo whistled. Beatings. This kid's life got worse and worse. "That's rough."

Lou grinned. "Yeah. But my last foster home really got to me. They went to church and prayed, but they also did devotionals every night. They gave things away to people, volunteered at places, and fixed food for other people all the time. They actually lived out the things they read."

"Humph. Not everyone does."

"I know. I scoffed at 'em every time. Who needed that? Wasting time on nothing more than a bunch of fairytales."

Bo squinted.

"Yeah. Now I'm reading the fairytales." Lou swung his legs

over the edge of the bed and his smile widened. "I lived with that family before I landed in here. I did everything I could to tick them off. I thought they'd eventually turn me back in and I wouldn't have to deal with their preaching anymore."

"And?"

"And they didn't. They grounded me. They took things away. But they never gave up on me. The last night there I snuck out with some buddies who robbed a liquor store. We got caught and I ended up here."

"So they finally gave up on you."

"That's the thing. They didn't. They have a bunch of other kids and live a few hours away, so they don't get to come visit. They write, though. They even came to all my hearings. And, they said they'll be there when I get out. I'll be transferred to real prison when I turn eighteen and should get out when I'm twenty. The state won't have anything to do with me then. But they'll be there."

Bo's brain stalled. He had nothing to say to that.

"When I first got arrested and thrown in here, I burned with anger. I blamed my friends. I blamed my useless biological parents. I blamed the foster system. Eventually, though, I had to accept my own responsibility. The longer I sat here, the more the things my foster family had said and read in here–" Lou picked up the Bible and tapped it. "–ran through my head. I beat myself up about what I did, but they told me I could change. I started going to the church services here and actually listened. Then I believed."

Bo scrunched up his nose. "You believe that stuff."

Lou leaned his head to the side. "Yeah. I do. I'm going to be locked up for a long time, but as long as I have this," he held the Bible up, "I'm free. They can't take away freedom that's on the inside."

Freedom on the inside? Lou'd been locked up too long. He'd become crazier than a diseased cow.

"I know. Crazy. But when you give it a chance, you'll see."

Bo grunted.

Lou's grin grew. "I know. But I'd rather be crazy and free on the inside than free on the outside and miserable."

"Yeah, well I'm not miserable."

"Right." Lou's expression challenged him.

Bo picked up the letter, put it back in the envelope, and slipped it under his mattress.

Chapter 27

Four days. Four days with no phone calls. No response from Mr. Wiser. Had he been called back to trial? Had the police laughed at her ideas?

Dana glanced at the computer screen one more time. She didn't know why she checked Facebook anymore. People posted the most ridiculous things. Who got drunk at the last party. Where the next party would be. Stupid sayings that meant nothing. Who hooked up with who.

Had she really considered these people her friends? None of them checked on her. Well, not none of them. She clicked on Crystal's name. She'd posted new pictures of her and Max, of them hanging out with his family. 'Day on the farm,' the caption read.

Brooke had new shots posted, too. She'd gone on a cruise with her parents and big sister who'd graduated from Sam Houston. Dana scanned the pictures. Beautiful blue skies, clear water, pools, bikinis, and drinks. *I can't believe she posted those.*

She clicked on Kara's profile next. 'Kara is now in a relationship with Jeremy Singer.'

"Wow. How'd I miss the official announcement?" Crystal's words from last week came back to her. *You've been…busy lately.* Had Dana really become that self-absorbed? Maybe she'd always been that self-absorbed.

When she had first moved there, she'd tried out for the cheerleading squad because she'd cheered at home and didn't want to be alone. She'd put everything into the squad until meeting Bo. Then she'd put everything into him. She'd started wearing Justin boots, going to rodeos, and listening to country music. He had become her world.

Now God held first place, but she still focused most of her energy on getting Bo home.

She was lucky she had any friends left. Clicking the "x" to close the window, she shut her computer down and shoved back her chair. She checked her phone as if a call from the lawyer would suddenly appear. It didn't. She paused as her hand went to slide it back into her pocket, she pulled it back out, flipped it open, and called Kara.

"Hello?"

"Hey, girl, it's me?"

"Me? Do I know a me?"

She plopped onto her bed. "I know. I haven't been exactly around lately. But I miss you. And I hear your summer's going pretty well."

"You could say that." She heard the grin in Kara's voice.

"So?"

"So…I'm at Jeremy's right now."

A dart pierced her heart. It should be the four of them hanging out. Maybe when Bo came home. The dart twisted. No. Not even then. It would be someone else hanging out with Kara, Jeremy, and Bo. She'd given him up. If she could just remember that. "Oh."

"He's home from his morning shift at the farm. He's working there again, part-time."

"Good. I'm glad he's back at work."

"What's this I hear about you not going to see Bo? How could you abandon him now?"

A hand flew to her throat. "I…haven't abandoned him. I have some stuff going on."

"More important than your boyfriend who's sitting in juvi? What could be more important than being there for him?"

God, that's what. 'I can't explain it right now. I haven't abandoned him. I've even talked to the lawyer about some things that might clear Bo."

"You've talked to the lawyer? About what?"

Now she'd said too much. She shouldn't have called. "Nothing I can talk about. Tell Jeremy I still love Bo and I'm trying to help him. I just can't go see him right now."

"Not even write him?"

"No," Dana squeaked.

"That makes no sense."

"I know. I do love him. And I think of him constantly." Too much.

"I still don't understand, but I'll tell him."

"Thanks."

"You sure you're okay?"

"Yeah." Dana didn't sound convincing even to herself. "I'm good. It just hurts that he's still in there. It feels like it's been forever already."

"I know. It should be only one more week though. Then that lawyer your parents got him can get him out."

"I hope so."

"We do, too. Hey, listen. I've got to go. Jeremy only has a few hours before he has to go back to work and he usually needs a nap in between."

"All right. I hope to see you soon."

"Ditto."

Dana jumped off the bed. She needed to get out of the house. She typed a message to Crystal. *"When r u going 2 Tyler mission again?"*

A few paces around her room later her phone chimed. *"Wed. U coming?"*

"Yes."

"Good. Max 2. Pick u up at 10."

"k."

That took care of Wednesday. But what would she do the next two days? Dana heard her mom in the kitchen. She guessed canning was better than going crazy. She tossed her phone on her bed and headed down the hall.

~ * ~

One new voice message. She hit send and punched in her password.

"Dana, this is Ray Wiser. I wanted to update you on what's going on with Bo's case. Give me a call when you get a chance."

On her third attempt, her fingers cooperated and dialed the lawyer's number.

"Ray Wiser here."

"Mr. Wiser, it's Dana Little."

"Yes, Dana. Thanks for returning my call. I've spoken with the police and frankly have gotten nowhere. They don't want to investigate any of your questions because it makes them look foolish. I didn't even tell them they came from you. But if they admit they should have looked into other theories, should have been looking for brake fluid, they'd also have to admit they were negligent in the investigation."

Her stomach tightened. "Okay. Now what?"

"Now we investigate on our own."

She liked this guy even more.

"I've contacted a private investigator I work with. He's in Dallas on a case right now, but he promised he'd be in touch before the end of the week."

That gave them almost no time. "But-"

"I know, court is next Monday. He knows that, too. He promised to get right on it, but can't come back to town for a couple of days. Worst case scenario we get a continuance."

"Can I…is there anything I can do before then?"

"Are you a praying person?"

The question shoved her down onto her bed. *Lately, it seemed a lot.* "Yes."

"Then pray. I'll call you when the P.I.'s in town."

"Okay, thanks."

She hung up the phone. Pray, pray, pray. Then listen. She fell to her knees and prayed every prayer she'd prayed over the last two and a half weeks all over again. Then she got quiet and listened.

~ * ~

Two days of making pickles and salsa. One day at the mission. Four days until court. Thursday was considered the end of the week, right?

Dana slowed to a walk and checked the caller ID when her phone sang. She took a swig of cold water from the bottle she held and wiped the sweat dripping down her face. She must be crazy running in this heat.

"Hello?"

"Dana, Ray Wiser. My investigator is here. His name is Jeff. Can you meet him at the Singer's house tomorrow?"

"Yes." She didn't mean to squeal her answer.

"Great. What time?"

"You tell me. I'll be there."

"Three?"

"Yes. He has the address?"

"He does. I'd like to be there, but I'll be in court wrapping up another case. He'll report his findings to me."

"Thanks Mr. Wiser. Thanks for believing in Bo." She hesitated, then plowed ahead. "And thanks for not treating me like a kid."

He chuckled. "Dana, you are no kid. You've proved that."

His words echoed in her head after she hung up. She picked up her pace and headed home, wondering what he meant. All she'd done was believe in her boyfriend and set out to prove his innocence. Anyone would do the same.

Chapter 28

Dana's hands shook as her tires crunched over the gravel-dirt mixed driveway. Jeff, the private investigator, should be there in fifteen minutes. She wanted to arrive early to see if anyone was home. Her heart sank when she saw Kara's car in her normal parking spot. She'd hoped everyone would be out.

She parked her car next to Kara's. *Stop shaking,* she demanded of her hands. *You've been here a million times. It's like home.*

Was like home.

Jeremy opened the door seconds after she knocked.

"Hey." Dana attempted a smile.

"Hey."

"Um, Kara's here?"

"Yeah. You looking for her?"

She shook her head. "Not really. I saw her car and thought I'd say hi."

Kara's brunette head popped out from behind Jeremy. "Hey."

"Hey." She slipped her hands in her back pockets.

"What's up, Dana?" Jeremy stood in the doorway, not moving to invite her in.

"I–" She cleared her throat. "I'm meeting a private investigator here."

Jeremy took a step back. "A private investigator?"

Kara's eyes grew round as a bale of hay.

"Yeah. I've been talking to the lawyer and we had some questions. The police refused to look into them, so he hired a P.I."

"*We* had some questions?"

"Yes, we. Anyway. I'm meeting the guy here so I can show him around."

"What are you showing him?" Jeremy hobbled over the threshold onto the porch. Kara followed, shutting the door behind her.

"Where Stacy parked. The driveway. Things like that."

"I want to be there. I was here, too, you know."

"I know." Dana swiped some hair out of her eyes.

An approaching car caught her attention. A black corvette pulled in and parked next to her car. Private investigating must pay well.

A big, football player-looking guy with curly black hair unfolded himself out of the car. He swaggered to the front porch and checked them out. His gaze landed on her. "You Dana?"

"I am."

He held his hand out and shook hers firmly. "Nice to meet ya. I'm Jeff." He looked beyond her. "And you are?"

Jeremy crossed his arms. "I'm Jeremy Singer. Bo's brother."

Recognition lit his face. "You're the dead girl's boyfriend."

"Her name was Stacy and I was her ex-boyfriend."

"Right." Jeff looked at Kara. "And you're the new girlfriend."

Kara held onto Jeremy's arm and nodded.

"Good. You were all here the day of the accident?"

"Yes," they replied in unison.

He pulled out a notebook and reviewed his notes. "Do I have everything right?"

"Yeah, pretty much," Jeremy answered.

"And how long did you and…" He checked his notes. "Stacy stay inside and talk?"

"I don't know. Ten minutes or so. I didn't time it."

"Of course." He looked at Dana. "And you were…?"

"Outside part of the time, then I went inside."

"Leaving Bo out here by himself."

"Yes."

"For how long?"

"Umm…" She scrunched up her nose. "Maybe five minutes or so. And he'd stomped off to the barn when I went in."

"But he was standing by the car when you came out with Stacy?"

"Yes." She'd relived that awful day too many times.

"He would've been taking an awful chance of no one coming out and catching him. He'd have had to scootch under the car, know exactly where the brake line lay, and jab it pretty hard to puncture it."

He didn't think Bo did it. *Oh, thank you, Lord. Now give us the rest.*

"Exactly." Jeremy limped down the steps. "He couldn't have done it and wouldn't have done it."

The right side of Jeff's lip curled up in a half smile. "That's what we intend to prove. Now, can you show me where Stacy parked her car that day?"

The group traipsed across the grass to the common parking area. Dana pointed. "She parked where my car is now."

"You mind moving it?"

"Sure." She pulled her keys out and moved her car to the other side of Jeff's. When she got out, he had some small glass containers in his hand.

"Right here?"

"Yes."

Jeff pulled a small camera out of his back pocket and took several pictures. He studied the ground, creeping over every inch of the area and taking several dirt samples and putting them in the containers he held. Finally, he stood. "Okay. The driveway I came in is the only way in and out?"

"Yup."

"All right. I'm going to do the same kind of thing down the driveway."

Dana gaped. "You know it's like a mile long."

The lopsided grin again. "I know. It wouldn't matter if it were five miles long. I do my job thoroughly." He pulled a marker from his car and labeled the containers. Then he pulled out a box full of more just like those he filled and marked. "What I need is someone to cover me. I don't want some unsuspecting parent or friend caught off guard by a man crouching in the driveway."

"I'll go."

"Me, too."

He examined the three of them. Dana looked at Jeremy and Kara. Kara hadn't said anything, but she hadn't loosened her grip on his arm either. Their faces mirrored the determination she felt. Her stomach somersaulted. They were so close. Dana wouldn't back down now. She had to know each and every detail.

"All right. We'll all go. But no questions. No interfering. And no doing your own snooping. I'm paid to be here and it's my job to do. Got it?"

Three heads bobbed.

He held the box out to Dana. "You carry these." He clipped the pen to his shirt and turned to Kara. "Think you can be in charge of taking pictures?"

"Sure."

"All right. Let's go."

'Let's go' turned out to mean 'let's creep down the mile long driveway inch by inch.'

Okay, maybe not inch by inch. Dana's arms began to ache from holding the box of slowly filled containers. But definitely foot by foot.

No one spoke as they crept down the driveway and Jeff filled the occasional glass container, labeled it, and returned it to the box. Sweat dripped down Dana's back and Jeremy swiped his forehead with his shirt sleeve several times. Kara snapped pictures every few minutes.

Dana counted thirteen filled containers when Kara whispered something in Jeremy's ear, handed him the small, blue camera, and headed back towards the house. *Guess she's escaping to the air conditioning.*

Jeff had just handed her the eighteenth container when Kara returned, dragging a wheeled cooler behind her.

"Thanks." Jeff downed his bottle of water in four gulps and handed the empty bottle back to Kara.

Dana sipped hers then rolled it on her neck. If they took much longer, the sun would go down. That would bring little relief from the scorching heat, though.

Jeff guzzled another sixteen point nine ounces of refreshment after handing Dana container number thirty-five. She rejoiced at seeing the main road as she drank the last swallow of her second bottle.

Almost done.

"Time to head back," Jeff announced as he handed Dana container number fifty. He took the camera from Kara and took pictures facing the whole walk back.

Once they arrived back at the cars, he took the box from Dana and set it on his hood. "Thanks. I'll have these looked at this weekend and hopefully we'll have something before trial Monday morning."

Her heart dropped to her stomach. "You…you can't tell anything? You didn't find anything that could help Bo?"

"I'm not sure. The dirt has to be examined by a lab. Luckily for your boyfriend, I have a forensic pathologist who owes me. He'll be putting in some long hours this weekend."

"Oh."

Jeff stuck out his hand and she shook it. "See you at the trial Monday."

Or not. The hearing brought a whole new onslaught of questions. She wanted to go, longed to, but knew she shouldn't. If Bo got released, it wouldn't be like she'd could run up to him and celebrate. She didn't even want to consider the possibility that he'd be convicted.

The vette's engine roared to life and crept back down the driveway almost as slow as they'd walked down it.

"Dana?"

She turned to Jeremy. "Yeah?"

"Thanks. First the lawyer and now this. I don't want to lose my brother, and I think you just saved his life."

"Jeremy, I love Bo. I really do. And I know he's innocent."

"I know. That's why I don't get–"

"It doesn't make sense, I know. I'll be able to explain after Monday. Tell Bo how much I love him, okay?"

"Sure."

Kara hugged Dana. "Thanks. It means everything to Jeremy."

A tear escaped and trickled down Dana's cheek as she nodded.

God, keep me going. Three more days. Then I have to break Bo's heart after what will hopefully be the best day of his life.

Chapter 29

Dana pushed the salad around on her plate, not able to bring a bite to her mouth.

Her mom reached over and patted her hand. "You okay, Dear?"

She shrugged her shoulders.

"Is it the trial tomorrow?"

She nodded.

"It'll be all right, Honey. Ray's the best. He won't let them get away with anything. Bo will be home this time tomorrow. I know it."

The fork explored the plate, not finding anything worth picking up. She pushed back her chair. "I can't eat. Thanks, though." She dumped the tossed vegetables into the trash, put her dishes in the sink and shuffled to her bedroom.

Her cell phone vibrated from its spot on the bed. Crystal.

"Hello?"

"Hey, girl. Wanted to give you a head's up. I've got some movies and I'll be there in twenty minutes."

"I don't think–" The phone went dead. She plopped onto her bed, burying her face in the pillows. *Lord, I know you're in charge. Let it be true. Let this nightmare be over tomorrow.*

Then a new nightmare would begin. Her life without Bo

permanently.

No. She pushed herself up. She'd made her decision. It had to be this way. If he couldn't accept God, she couldn't be with him. Period.

So why did her heart cry out in protest?

Her phone buzzed again. Katherine. *"Coming ur way. Have lots of junk food & tissues."*

Dana's fingers flew over the keys. *"It's ok. Crystal's coming w/ movies. I'm good."*

"I know. C u soon."

A grin snuck onto her lips. She'd spend the rest of her life paying those two back for their friendship over the last three weeks.

After washing her face, Dana waited for the bombardment on her bedroom floor reading her Bible. She looked up from Psalm fifteen when someone banged on her door.

"Hey, girl." Crystal burst in sporting a stack of movies, as promised. "I've got sappy, silly, science fiction, and suspense. What do you feel like?" She plopped on the floor.

"Not suspense. I've had enough of that in real life lately, thank you."

Her laugh rang loud as she looped her arm through Dana's. "You've had enough sappy, too. Will it be silly or science fiction."

"Ugh. Not science fiction, please," another voice added.

Katherine entered the room loaded down with grocery bags.

Crystal smiled. "Silly, it is." She tossed the other videos on Dana's bed. "Whatcha got?"

Katherine peaked into one of the plastic sacks. "Twizzlers, M & M's, Gobstoppers, Riesens, and movie theatre popcorn."

"Oh." Dana put a hand on her jaw. "I think I feel the cavity forming already."

Crystal raised her eyebrows. "I think our girl still has her sense of humor."

"Yep."

Katherine plopped down on Dana's other side. "But, I brought these just in case." She pulled out three boxes of tissue from the other bag.

"Three boxes? The trial's tomorrow, you know. I couldn't use three boxes in a day and a half if I tried."

"Hmm. Maybe we'll find another use for them." Crystal winked.

"Yeah, right." Dana detangled herself and stood. "If we're going to watch a movie, let's go do it. You two have gotten downright weird."

Plunked on the couch, sandwiched between her friends, Dana ignored the candy. She didn't think her stomach could take sweets, or anything else.

~ * ~

"Another one?" Crystal held up a DVD case. "It's not silly, but it's still early."

"No, two's enough."

"Now what?" Crystal replaced the disk from the player back in its case and sat beside Dana, curling her legs underneath her. "And don't even try to tell me you're going to bed at eight-thirty."

"Yeah." Katherine's voice softened. "What are you going to do tomorrow."

"Sit and wait."

"What do you mean you'll be sitting and waiting? At the trial, right next to us, right?"

Dana pulled her ponytail out and redid it. She sighed. "No. I won't be there."

Crystal stood and faced her. "Have you lost your mind? Why wouldn't you go? After everything you've done for Bo? If he gets off tomorrow, it'll most likely be because of you."

"You know why, Crystal. I can't be with Bo. I'm not going to the trial to watch him get released and then hug him and say, what? 'Congratulations, but now I have to break up with you'? That'd work well."

Crystal paced. "Well, I…I mean look at Max. He's been going to church with me. He's become a Christian and is getting baptized. You never know."

"Yeah, but you haven't been dating that long. Bo and I have been together forever. And he's mad at God. He got mad at me every time I even brought up going to church. I refuse to fake that everything's okay. I told him I love him and I mean it. I've done everything I can for him. I'll explain the rest later. After he's had his day."

Crystal dropped onto the couch. "Oh, you're right. But it feels like you should be there."

"I know. But I've made my decision."

Katherine's quiet voice broke in. "Then I'll stay here with you."

"And I'll go for you. I'll text you every detail."

"No." Dana shook her head. "That'll be worse. Besides, I don't think you can take your phone into the court room. I'll wait. The only thing that matters is the verdict."

"Okay. Then I'll text you right after."

She nodded and Katherine laid a hand on her arm. "Let's pray."

Chapter 30

"You need to eat something," Katherine insisted.

"I'll be fine. Doesn't the Bible say something about fasting and praying?"

"Is that what you call it?"

"Haven't we been praying? Well, I'm fasting, too."

Katherine's pursed lips told Dana she hadn't convinced her.

"I'm fine. I promise." She glanced at her phone. "It can't be that much longer, can it?"

~ * ~

Bo watched as Ray Wiser stood and walked towards the witness stand. "Officer Becker, did you go to Mr. Singer's house on May twenty-ninth?"

The young officer on the stand sat up straight and held his chin high. "I did."

"And did you question Mr. Bo Singer in reference to Stacy Athens' car accident?"

"I did."

"At that time, did you believe that Mr. Bo Singer had caused Miss Athens' accident?"

Officer Becker cleared his throat. "We had only begun our

investigation."

"So, you didn't think Mr. Bo Singer punctured Miss Athens' brake line."

"As I said, we were beginning our investigation."

Ray checked his notes. "And did you arrest Mr. Singer only two days later?"

"I did." Officer Becker nodded towards the prosecutor's table. "My partner Wells and I did."

"And Officer Wells had gone to the Singer's residence on May twenty-ninth also?"

"Yes."

"And he also questioned Mr. Bo Singer?"

"Yes."

"Did you question anyone else that day?"

"We talked with Mr. Jeremy Singer and a girlfriend."

"Dana Little."

"Yes. That sounds right."

"And did Mr. Jeremy Singer or Miss Dana Little lead you to believe that Mr. Bo Singer had caused Miss Athens' accident?"

"Both the witnesses admitted that Bo Singer had been outside by himself on the day of the accident before Miss Athens left."

"At any time did you verify how long Mr. Bo Singer had been outside by himself with Miss Athens' car?"

Officer Becker squirmed. "I'd have to read my notes to be sure."

"Let me refresh your memory." Ray picked up a slip of paper and read from it. "Mr. Bo Singer said he hadn't been alone with Miss Athens' car. Miss Dana Little reported that when she and Miss Athens exited the house, Mr. Bo Singer stood by the car."

"That sounds right."

"I hope so. It's what you wrote in the official report." Ray tossed the paper on the table where Bo sat. "So, you never asked how long Mr. Bo Singer had been outside by himself?"

"No. I didn't need to."

"Is that because you'd already decided Mr. Bo Singer was guilty?"

"No."

"Hmm. So, Mr. Bo Singer could have been outside by himself for five minutes, twenty minutes, or an hour. You don't really know."

"According to the information we gathered, we felt he had enough time to damage Miss Athens' car."

"You felt he had enough. Interesting." Ray picked up another piece of paper. "Did you or Officer Wells at any time collect any physical evidence from the scene of the accident or the Singer's property?"

"We had Miss Athens' car. That's how we knew the brake line had been punctured."

"Did anyone examining Miss Athens' car report wear and tear on the brake line? Whether it'd been compromised?"

"Um, no. That wasn't mentioned."

Mr. Wiser pulled a large photo from a folder on the table. "Your Honor, I'd like to reference exhibit G, which the prosecution has already entered into evidence. I've blown up the picture of Miss Athens' brake line and the puncture in question."

The judge nodded. "Proceed, counselor."

"Officer Becker, do you recognize this picture?"

He examined the photo. "Yes, it's a blow up of one in evidence, like you said."

"Do you notice anything about the line around the puncture?"

Officer Becker squinted. "I'm not sure. I'm not a car expert."

Mr. Wiser returned to the table and snatched up another sheet of paper. "No, but I did talk to an expert. Your Honor, I'd like to enter into evidence a statement from a seasoned mechanic that the red and black specks on the line are evidence of wear and tear that naturally occurs as vehicles age. Wear and tear that could make the line compromised and vulnerable."

Officer Becker's face reddened.

"Objection." The prosecuting attorney stood. "We don't have any verification of this statement or the expertise of this witness. Nor was this submitted to the prosecution ahead of time."

"We didn't get the blow up and talk to our expert until this weekend. If you check with a clerk in your office, I'm sure you'll find a fax waiting for you."

"We still don't know anything about this so-called specialist."

"Mr. Wiser, is your witness available to testify in person

about their qualifications and findings?"

"He is, Your Honor."

"I'll allow it."

Mr. Wiser handed the form to the judge and turned to face Officer Becker once again.

"You never closely examined the brake line past observing the puncture. Did you collect dirt samples? Look for brake fluid that would have certainly began leaking out as soon as the line was punctured?"

"No. We saw no need."

"Also interesting. Did you examine the Singer's driveway to see if anything large and sharp impeded the road?"

"We had no trouble driving down the driveway."

"How fast would you say you drove down the Singer's driveway?"

"I don't know. Five, maybe ten miles an hour."

"Didn't Miss Little report that Miss Athens sped from the house?"

His face reddened. "Yes."

"Isn't it possible something wouldn't be a problem at five miles an hour, but could be a problem at thirty or forty?"

"There wasn't anything in the driveway."

"Did you ask the Singer's if they had cleared the driveway? If any debris from the trees lining their mile-long drive had fallen recently and subsequently been removed?"

"No."

"Hmm." Ray rustled more papers before looking up. "No further questions."

When he cross examined Officer Wells, Ray gave him the same treatment. And received the same answers.

Bo no longer had to remind himself to sit up straight. Ray Wiser had fully captured his attention and sent his heart thudding with hope. He made it sound so simple. The police didn't have enough evidence.

The despair he'd felt after a handful of his peers testified how he'd sworn his hatred of Stacy began to melt.

He really did have a chance of going home today.

But where was Dana? He'd searched for her everywhere. When he'd caught Jeremy's eye, his brother had shaken his head. She didn't come. Had no plans to come. Hadn't written him or come to see him since her final letter. But Jeremy swore she declared she still loved him and even had a private investigator come out to the house to help clear him of these bogus charges.

So why wasn't she there?

The questions droned on. The ones in Bo's head and the ones from the prosecutor and Mr. Wiser. Ray, he'd told Bo to call him. He'd have to rethink his feelings about lawyers.

He focused on the witness stand when Ray called his first witness: Jeff Ark.

"Can you state your name and profession for the court, please?"

"Jeffrey Ark. I'm a private investigator."

"Thank you, Mr. Ark. Have you ever met the defendant, Mr. Bo Singer before."

"Never seen him before today." He nodded his head. "Pleasure to meet you."

Bo grinned. This guy wasn't too bad either.

"What brings you here today, Mr. Ark?"

"Jeff." He rolled his eyes. "Please don't call me Mr. Ark. And *you* brought me here today, *Mr.* Wiser."

"How long have we known each other, Jeff?"

"Oh, going on ten years, I'd say."

"And have you worked on other cases for me?"

"A few."

"Have you always found information that helped my client?"

Jeff's lips curled up on the right side. "Not always."

"When did you begin investigating on Mr. Bo Singer's case?"

"Friday."

"Friday…?"

"Last Friday. Like three days ago."

"June twenty-first of this year?"

"Yes. If that's the date of last Friday.'"

Ray smiled. "It was. Could you tell the court what your investigation entailed?"

"I visited the Singer's property. I spoke with a Mr. Jeremy Singer, Miss Dana Little, and Miss Kara O'Brien."

"Is that all?"

Jeff leaned back in the chair. "No."

"What else did your investigation consist of?"

"I collected sixty-eight vials of dirt from the Singer property."

"And why did you do that?"

"You asked me to."

"Why did I ask you to?"

"To have the soil tested for brake fluid."

Ray looked at the jury. His gaze returned to Jeff. "Was it a stretch that brake fluid would be found a month after Miss Athens' accident?"

"Yes and no. Time and travel over the road would definitely disrupt any deposits. Rain would also almost definitely wash away any trace left after other travel."

"To your recollection, has it rained in the last month?"

"Not a drop. My mom complains every day that all her flowers are dying. She made me buy her drip hoses to water her flower beds."

"I'm sorry to hear about your mom's flowers. But that's good for increasing the chances that any leaked fluid might still be found."

"It is."

"And can you tell the court what testing of those sixty-eight vials of dirt taken from the Singer's property showed?"

The prosecutor leapt to his feet. "Objection. Entering new evidence. We know nothing of this testing or its results."

Ray strode back to his table and grabbed some papers. "We didn't get the soil samples until Friday of last week, June twenty-first. The results from the lab came in last night around six p.m. While you have someone checking on the fax about the blown up picture, you'll also find a copy of these results. But, I brought extra copies just in case." He handed a packet of papers to the prosecutor and to the judge. "Your Honor, I'd like to enter the soil lab results as exhibit Q."

"They'll be so entered." He accepted the packet and flipped through it.

The prosecutor tossed his copy on the desk. "Your Honor, we have no way to validate these results. We don't know anything about the lab that performed the tests or the credibility of the forensic technician."

Ray clasped his hands together. "Your Honor, the lab

information is located on the results and we have the technician who performed the tests here ready to testify to his credibility."

The judge glared at the prosecutor. "If you'd wanted a chance to refute physical evidence and lab tests, your officers should have gathered it themselves. Objection overruled."

Bo almost jumped out of his seat. This was good. Very, very good.

He didn't know the test results yet, though. But Ray wouldn't have brought it up if it wouldn't help him. He leaned forward.

"Now, Mr…um Jeff. Could you tell us what the lab results showed about the soil you collected?"

"Sure. Of the sixty-eight vials, twelve of them contained the chemical combination found in brake fluid." He looked at Bo. "And forty of them contained the chemical combination found in anti-freeze. Someone needs to inspect their car before they find themselves stranded on the side of the road."

"Twelve of the sixty-eight. That's not many. Can you tell us where on the property the twelve samples containing brake fluid were found?"

"All twelve vials came from more than four hundred yards from where Miss Athens parked her car."

"Four hundred yards." Ray scribbled. "So, that's about a quarter mile."

"About."

"How many vials of soil did you take where Miss Athens parked?"

"Eighteen."

"And none of those soil samples showed traces of brake fluid?"

"Not one of them."

"Does that prove that Miss Athens' car didn't start leaking brake fluid where she'd parked it?"

"No. It doesn't prove it. But it makes me doubt seriously that her car began leaking before the four hundred yards down the driveway where brake fluid was found."

"Thank you, Mr. Ark."

Bo attempted to listen as the prosecutor questioned Jeff. When it became obvious he couldn't shake him, Bo began imagining sleeping in his bed that night. Being home. Eating his mom's cooking. Seeing Dana.

Maybe seeing her. That one still confused him.

He listened as Ray and the prosecutor questioned the lab tech. His answers sounded like heaven to Bo's ears.

Ray had planned to call Dana to testify Bo hadn't had enough time to damage Stacy's car, but said he didn't need to since he'd gotten the P.I. and lab guy.

He offered to call in the car expert. The prosecutor declined and Ray closed his case.

Bo glanced back at his family. They beamed. They'd been glum when they'd arrived, trying to hide it behind grimaces, but he knew them too well. Now, he saw the hope he felt reflected on their faces.

The judge stood and adjourned the court. He'd call the lawyers back when he reached a decision. The man holding Bo's entire fate and future in his hands had his full attention. Had he been convinced? Did he doubt that Bo could have done what he was accused of, and doubt it enough to let him go home?

He hoped so, because it was all he had to hang on to.

Chapter 31

Bo stood next to Ray. He rubbed his sweaty palms on his pants. He hoped, but he also doubted. Never did he think he'd find himself accused of murder. That meant anything was possible. Even getting convicted.

Ray said the judge coming back in only an hour most likely meant not guilty. There's no way he'd convict a kid of murder that quickly.

"After reviewing the evidence provided and the witness testimonies, I have come to a solid verdict."

Bo gripped the table in front of him. The gray-haired man held his entire fate and took his time revealing it. "I'm very disappointed in the lack of extensiveness of the investigation in this case. We should not conclude a person's guilt before looking into all possibilities, which is what I believe happened here.

"I am unable to find beyond a reasonable doubt that Mr. Singer caused the damage to Miss Athens' car. Therefore, on the count of First Degree Murder, I find the defendant, Bo Manning Singer, not guilty."

Bo's ears buzzed as the court erupted. Not guilty! They believed him. Or at least they'd believed Mr. Wiser and Jeff Ark. He'd go home today. Free.

The judge pounded his gavel and said something else, but it

didn't register with Bo. He'd heard the only thing he needed to hear. His mom wrapped her arms around his neck and Jeremy cupped Bo's hand in his. Tears glistened in his dad's eyes. Other familiar faces swarmed before him. His friends and family, minus one.

~ * ~

Dana's phone buzzed. She looked at Katherine. "I can't look."

"Do you want me to look?"

"Yes." She held the phone out. "No." She yanked it back. "Once I see it there's no going back. It's done."

"It's done either way, Dana."

"You're right. I'll look." Her phone buzzed again. "That's a good sign. Right?"

"It has to be."

"Okay. Here goes." She peeked at her phone.

"Not guilty!!!"

"Yes." She fell to her knees. "Thank You, Lord. Thank You, thank You, thank You!"

~ * ~

Bo's daze hadn't faded two hours later when he saw his home come into view from the back seat of his dad's truck. He soaked it all in. Home. Fields. Horses. He stepped out of the car and inhaled the familiar smells of the farm. Hay. Manure. Home.

The yard filled with cars before he made it to the front porch. Food covered the dining table and kitchen counters. Congratulations and pats on the back surrounded him. Jeremy leaned against the doorframe between the dining room and den, grinning.

Hours later, the last few guests trickled out the door to be greeted by the stars twinkling and crickets chirping. Bo looked longingly at the barn. Tomorrow. Tonight he wanted a shower in his own bathroom and a good night's sleep in his own bed.

Clean and ready for bed, he said goodnight to his folks and Jeremy, accepting the millionth kiss from his mom. He shut the door, wrapped himself in familiarity, lay back, and reached for his phone. It alerted him to more than thirty new messages when he turned it on. Scrolling through, he found the only one that interested him. Dana had sent it at three o'clock. Right after the verdict.

"Bo, I'm on my knees grateful. I knew they couldn't convict u. Love u always. Don't ever 4get. Will come over 2morrow."

She'd texted him. Said she loved him. His heart should relax. But the other words haunted him. On her knees grateful? What did that mean? And why would she tell him not to forget she loved him?

His freedom and being in his own bed proved to be the cure for the knots that had taken up residence in his stomach. The serpent around his heart, though, that remained.

~ * ~

Dana inched up the driveway. She'd never dreaded coming here. Not even the day she met the P.I. had she been so nervous. Her stomach had flipped somersaults all morning. She'd managed to get some cinnamon toast down, the first thing she'd eaten since breakfast Sunday. Maybe after breaking Bo's heart she would be able to eat again.

The roller coaster dip from within told her differently.

The modest farmhouse with a wide front porch and thin, square columns came into view. This would be the last time she'd come here. She parked next to Kara's car and stepped out, drinking in the sight.

Don't hug him. Don't even touch him. You'll never want to let go.

She took two steps toward the house and stopped when Bo came through the front door. His black cowboy hat sat atop his head with wild curls escaping around it. His wranglers showed off his toned legs and she knew all too well the muscles his shirt hid. She met his gaze and held it.

He sauntered across the porch and down the steps.

She sprinted across the grass, flung her arms around his neck, and held tight as he wrapped his arms around her waist and spun her in circles. She let his lips cover hers and came away breathless.

"Dana, it feels so good to have you in my arms. I didn't think … I didn't know what to think."

She sucked in the air between them. His words splashed cold. She'd lost control. But one more embrace, one more kiss. She'd cherish them forever. Now, she had to break his heart. She stepped back. "Let's go for a walk."

They strolled hand in hand to the barn. Dana ached to forget every promise she made to herself and to God and wrap herself in his warmth once again.

God, she couldn't do this.

I can do all things through Christ who strengthens me.

She never thought those words would cause pain for someone she loved. Her past mistakes had gotten her there. Now she needed to make the right decision.

She led them to the familiar stump between the barn and the far fence. She pulled him down on it and turned to face him and withdrew her hand from his.

"Bo, I." She swallowed. "I don't know where to begin."

He examined her. "Now I'm really confused. One minute you're all over me and now you don't know where to begin?"

"I love you, Bo. I do. I'll never stop loving you."

"But?"

"But some things have changed. I've changed."

His jaw tightened. "Is there someone else? I bet Chet stepped it up with me out of the picture."

Dana grimaced. "I only ran into him once. If you and every other man in Texas got locked up and Chet was the only one around, I'd stay single. And no. There's no one else. Not exactly."

"Not exactly?"

"There's not another guy. No one could compare to you." She resisted the urge to caress his stubbly cheek.

Bo took his hat off, ran his hand through his hair, and replaced it. "Then what?"

"I started working on my relationship with God before they arrested you. You know that."

Bo stood. "*That* again."

"Yes, that. With you gone, I searched what I believed and spent my time figuring out what God wants for me."

"And?"

"He wants me. To dedicate my life to Him. To love Him."

"Okay."

"You don't love God, Bo. You're not even sure you believe

in Him. How does that fit with me going to church two or three days a week and regularly volunteering at a homeless shelter?"

His green eyes grew stormy. "It won't."

"That's what I thought." Dana swallowed down the threatening tears. She stood and put her hand on his arm. He flinched. "I love you, Bo. I did everything I could to help get you home. I hope you know that. But I have to put God first. He never gave up on me, even when I'd given up on Him."

The storm in Bo's eyes brought moisture. "You're leaving me for a fairytale."

"It's not a fable, Bo. God's real. He loves you, too. There's a reason He let you get arrested. And a reason He brought you back home."

"A reason? That was the worst experience of my life."

"I know. But He can bring good out of it. He's waiting for you. If you ever find Him, I'll be waiting, too." She stepped towards him and his body stiffened. "I'll never stop loving you."

She turned on her heel and fled to her car. Tears streamed down her face as she left the Singer's property for the last time.

Chapter 32

God! Bo threw a blanket over his favorite horse. He was losing the best thing that ever happened to him because of God.

Dana's words stomped around in his head. They mixed with the things Lou had told him. Sandy Bridges stepped away from him as he pulled the saddle strap too tight.

"Sorry, girl." He patted the mare's neck.

God loves you. God's waiting for you. I used to scoff, too. Then I believed. Lou's words haunted him.

Bo led Sandy Bridges out of the barn and mounted her. At least now he could pound out his thoughts through hooves racing across open fields.

When he brought Sandy back and cooled her down, his thoughts still spun. And his heart felt like it'd been on a day-long bull ride. He didn't like emotions. How could he be feeling so many at one time?

Brushing Sandy down, he decided. He'd lived his life before Dana and he'd live it fine after her.

~ * ~

This is not living. Bo stared into the dark. Crickets chirped and frogs croaked. No light invaded his room. Or his heart. He'd been home four days. Free from concrete and guards and schedules. His heart was trapped, though. He'd been fine before Dana because he didn't know that kind of love. She'd taught him. Filled him with love and then yanked it away leaving a gaping hole.

What had Lou said about being locked up on the outside but being free on the inside? Now Bo had the opposite.

He'd always hated God. Hated what God made his grandfather do to his dad. No loving God would let that happen. Especially by someone who supposedly preached His word.

Dana was different, though. And Lou. They did what they said. They had something special, but he couldn't put his finger on it.

He believed Dana loved him. He couldn't wrap his mind around why she'd leave him if she loved him, but deep down, he knew she did. For the last four days, he'd blamed God. Now he desperately wanted to figure out how to get her back.

He groaned. The only way to do that was to figure out this God thing.

Okay, God. If You're out there, prove it.

~ * ~

The concrete walls taunted Bo. He never thought he'd find himself back at this place. He slammed his car door and strode to the entrance. The building had no hold over him anymore. But it might hold the answer he looked for.

He emptied his pockets and signed in as a visitor. Familiar guards raised their eyebrows as they led him to the visitor area. He took in the smell of Clorox and said another silent 'thank you' that he would walk back out of this place in less than an hour.

To who?

The question caught him off guard.

Who was he thanking?

He rubbed his hands together. He thanked Dana. And Ray. And even Jeff. They're the ones that got him off. Right?

Bo stood when Lou walked in and shook his hand.

"Man, I didn't think I'd ever see you again."

"Yeah, well, I couldn't stay away."

Lou's grin lit up his face. "I'm sure. It's good to see you, but what's up?"

"I wanted to ask you about something."

"Shoot."

"Dana…" Bo lost his question.

"The girlfriend."

Bo cleared his throat. "She apparently pestered my lawyer and got him to get a private investigator to help get me off."

Lou whistled. "That's some girlfriend."

"Then when I got home, she broke up with me."

"Huh?"

"That's what I said. And she swears she still loves me."

Lou scrunched his eyebrows. "I never did understand women."

Bo chuckled. "Me either."

"So what's your question?"

"When she broke up with me, she said she did it because of God. Her life involves church now and that stuff wouldn't fit with me being in her life anymore."

"I see. The good ole unequally yoked."

"The what?"

"The Bible guides Christians not to marry people who aren't believers. God actually told the Jews not to marry outside their faith long before, also."

"So it *is* God's fault she broke up with me."

"Yes. And no. God did say it. She made the choice to do it."

"She said she'd be waiting for me if I found God. I want to know what made you decide to believe that stuff you read."

"The ultimate question. Is God real and does He really want to have a relationship with you?" Lou folded his hands on the table and leaned in. "For me, seeing people live out what they said went a long way. Having someone love me despite doing everything I could to push them away. Then I read the Bible for myself. I found the God behind their love and decided to love Him back."

"It sounds too simple."

Lou leaned back. "It is simple."

"I don't know."

"What do you believe about God?"

"I'm not sure. It just seems crazy."

"Tell me about your horses."

Bo narrowed his eyes at the sudden change in topic. Was

Lou trying to trick him? "We have five of them. They're beautiful, majestic. And strong."

"You love them?"

Bo cocked his head to the side. He'd never thought of it that way. "I guess."

"You take care of them? Feed them? Exercise them?"

"Yeah."

"If one's sick, do you call the vet and give it medicine?"

"Yeah." Where was he going?

"How'd you get those horses?"

"Three of them we bought. Two of them were foaled on our farm."

"So you paid a price for them."

"Yeah."

"You didn't create them, though. Didn't do anything to make them?"

"No, of course not."

"Still, you're willing to sacrifice your time and energy for them."

"Yes. What are you getting at?"

Lou smirked. "I'll get there. One more question. If one of your horses got stranded in a raging river, would you risk your life to save it?"

"In a heartbeat."

"Then why is it so crazy that God, who created you would love you, want a relationship with you, and even be willing to sacrifice His Son for you?"

Bo fell back in his chair. "Whoa."

He'd never thought about it like that. If God did exist, did create people, wouldn't He do that? Bo would risk his life for a horse. What Lou said, what Dana believed in, wasn't any more crazy.

"Exactly."

"But I'm not even sure if I believe God exists. If He does, I might could buy that. If he exists, why's He let so many bad things happen?"

"Now it gets deep. If God doesn't exist, how'd we get here?"

"Evolution. The big bang. You know, all that."

"I know it's a theory that people like to say really happened.

You believe that you once came from ameba? That your blood system that works with your oxygen system and feeds all your muscles and organs, which are held up by your bones all evolved independently of each other and somehow gravitated towards each other over millions of years, even though each one of those systems depends on the other to work?"

"I never thought about it."

"How exactly would skin develop to cover everything when everything can't survive without the protection of skin? And why would skin develop without anything to protect?"

"Huh. It doesn't make sense."

Lou tapped his fingers together. "To me it doesn't. Neither does a theory that says life forms have transitioned to what they are now over millions of years. Wouldn't there be millions, or even thousands of fossils for scientists to put on display as proof?"

"I'd think so. They have all the pictures in science books."

Lou grinned. "Right. Pictures that are drawn. How many pictures of actual fossils have you seen?"

Bo sat up. He'd never paid that much attention in school, but he did remember the little picture of a fish growing legs and lungs. No bones. No fossils. Just drawings. He'd never realized that before. "None."

"Exactly. Even Darwin himself acknowledged this was a serious problem in his theory. And it hasn't changed in a hundred and fifty years."

"That's not exactly how evolution's taught."

"No kidding." Lou's grin widened. "I've had quite a bit of time to do my own research the last few months. When I combined what I've learned with the love of God I've seen in people around me, I believed."

Bo's heart thudded. It went against everything he'd ever thought. Could it be true? He tried to wrap his mind around the idea of a real God who might love him.

The boa constrictor squeezing his heart loosened its grip. He met Lou's eyes. "Tell me more."

Chapter 33

Dana laughed at her dad's attempt to wakeboard. She rarely saw him out of a business suit, much less in swim shorts and strapped to a board on the water. It still amazed her that he'd confessed he skied almost every weekend of his childhood. His parents had died before Dana was born and her dad always worked long hours, eliminating his connections to the water and time to play on it.

Her dad climbed into the boat dripping wet and out of breath. Dana giggled and looked across the lake. The water provided welcome relief from the scorching July sun. She'd been soaking it in on the boat of her parents' friends since lunch. Their kids were older, married and doing their own thing.

She leapt into the water and floated on a life jacket. Hanging out with the folks proved to be better than she'd thought. The lake and boat helped tremendously.

Bo entered her thoughts. She did what she'd trained herself to do whenever his handsome face popped up.

Lord, I want him back. Bring him to You so that can happen. Or take my wanting him away.

"You ready to try the wakeboard, Dana?" Her mom motioned to the dripping board laid out on the swim platform.

"Seriously?"

"If your dad can try it, so can you."

"Okay." She shoved off her thoughts of Bo once again and grabbed the board.

~ * ~

Dana wrapped a towel around her. She'd done it. It'd taken five or six tries, but she'd finally gotten up on the wakeboard. Now her legs ached and threatened to give out.

"We're heading back to the cabin to start the grill. Everyone's getting hungry."

"I'm famished." Dana collapsed into the seat.

While her dad and his friend stacked charcoal and doused it with lighter fluid, Dana went to take a shower. She checked her phone as she grabbed her clothes.

"Hey, girl. Happy 4th. Cu Sunday."

Katherine. Dana typed of her reply. *"Thx. U2. Enjoy the fireworks. Love you lots."*

The message envelope appeared on the home screen.

Two unread ones sat in her inbox.

One from Crystal. *"Going 2 meet M…"* The rest of the message waited for her to click on it to read. The text below stopped her from clicking on Crystal's message.

Bo. Her heart took off like a race horse. *"Want 2 talk 2 u…"* She scrolled down and clicked.

"Want 2 talk 2 u. Have something to tell u. Where r u 2day? Will come to u."

Her heart pounded as she ran through the possibilities of what the text could mean. Had something happened? Did Jeremy have a relapse with his leg? No. He could text that. Or call her. If he even bothered telling her. He'd been so mad when she left last Tuesday. Did he want to tell her off in person? Maybe he'd been stewing over her words, coming up with the right comeback.

Bo wouldn't do that. He'd simmer in silence for a year without saying a word. She read the text again and her hope soared, jumping over every barrier, every doubt that came to mind. If only her biggest desire had just been answered: Bo had found God. It seemed impossible.

Nothing is impossible with God.

Her fingers flew. *"At Lake Mattern w/folks. 3324 Hampton*

Drive. Will b here through fireworks. Home 2morrow. Want 2 meet then?"

Her phone buzzed. *"No. B there in hour."*

"Oh, God. Is it true? Can I really have You and Bo?"

She glanced at her phone again, tossed it on the bed, grabbed her clothes, and danced on her way to the shower.

~ * ~

Bo wouldn't care if she wore makeup or not, but putting it on helped her pass the time. Dana brushed her hair. No rumble of his Mustang coming down the road.

Once outside, the smell of charcoal and grilled burgers made her stomach growl. Her parents and their friends stood around with several other neighbors. A few young kids milled around and a boy about her age twirled some of them around. They treated him like a moving jungle gym.

She grabbed a plate and filled it from the bowls and glass dishes lined up on several plastic white tables that had been pushed together. She stood at one end and filled a cup with sweet tea. Turning to go find a place to sit, she almost ran into jungle gym boy.

Dana balanced her plate. "Sorry. Didn't know you were there."

The tall, lanky boy grinned. "No problem. My name's Mark. I haven't seen you around the lake before."

"I'm Dana. My parents' friends own this place. It's my first time here."

"That explains it. Did you have a good day?"

The corners of Dana's lips turned up. "It's been fun."

"Then you might come back one day."

"I suppose…" Her heart sped up. Something felt off. She spun around and spotted Bo standing by the corner of the house. His jaw twitched and he turned to leave. "Bo."

"What'd you say?"

"Nothing." She shoved her plate and cup at Mark. "Here. Hold this." He took them and she darted after Bo.

He opened his car door as she reached the driveway. "Bo, wait!"

He looked at her with sad eyes. "You knew I was coming, Dana. What was that? Did you want me to see you with someone else so I'd leave you alone?"

"Did I…" She looked back at the house, then met Bo's gaze. "No. He walked up to me to introduce himself. He's a neighbor and I just met him. And I'm *not* interested."

Bo's hand fell off the door handle. "You're not?"

"No. Not even the teeniest, weeniest bit." She closed the space between them in three steps.

"That's good."

She fought against the urge to hold his hand, wrap him in a hug. Anything. But she knew it'd be the end of her resolve is she did. She had to see what he'd come to say. "So, you had something you wanted to tell me?"

Bo closed his door and leaned against it. "I've been thinking."

She held her breath.

"And I talked to Lou."

"Lou?"

"Yeah. My roommate."

"At juvi?"

"Yeah. He's a Christian."

"Oh?"

"He explained a few things to me." Bo reached for her hand.

She let him take it and sparks flew up her arm straight to her heart.

"I get it, Dana. I believe."

"Believe what exactly." She had to be sure. Couldn't get sucked back into her love for Bo only to have it snatched away again.

"I believe God exists and loves me. I believe He wants a relationship with me and sent Jesus to pay for my sins because I never could."

"Really? You're not saying it so we can be together again?"

"No. I considered it." Bo laughed. "But Lou talked me out of it. And talked me into real faith."

Dana beamed. "I've got to meet this Lou."

"You will, one day. I still have lots of questions to ask him."

She fell against his chest and arms wrapped around her. Was it real? He'd truly given his life to God?

She looked up, meeting his eyes. The anger had

disappeared. The hatred no longer clouded his gorgeous green eyes.

Bo kissed the top of her head. "So you'll have me back, imperfections and all?"

She could hardly breathe. "As long as those imperfections come with faith, absolutely."

"They do." His husky voice reassured her. Of his new-found faith, and deep love for her.

She brushed his lips with hers and pulled back in wonder.

Thank You, God. You really do perform miracles.

Dear Reader,

I hope you've enjoyed reading Dana's story. She is a girl full of heart and I had a great time getting to know her and telling her story. While she is a fictional character and her story is too, her struggles with love and faith are real ones that many of us find ourselves working through.

Bo's difficulty coming to terms with God after experiencing someone dishing out abuse in His name is also a very real challenge many people face. Hopefully Bo and Lou's discussion has equipped you with a bit more information about the evidences for God and possibly act as a catalyst to search for even more of that evidence, which is available in abundance.

I would love to hear what you thought of Dana's story. Reviews on Amazon are always welcome! I'd also be honored to hear your story. I believe everyone has a story and there are elements of each of our lives that can be told in a way that overflows blessings to others. If you would like your story considered for the telling in this format, I invite you to contact me via my website.

Gratefully,

Tracy Wainwright

www.tracywainwright.com

Acknowledgements

First, I have to acknowledge the Lord for His pouring out of His Spirit to save me and then call me to a life I never imagined. To gift me the ability, desire, and joy in writing is a true miracle that I'm abundantly grateful for.

Next, I want to thank my husband and children who are so patient with me when I dive into a book and am in writing mode. I can't thank you enough for the graciousness when no dinner is cooked, laundry sits around for days, and clutter builds up in piles, nor for being my eagle eyes.

I also want to acknowledge the inspiration for Dana's story. It was a beautiful warm spring day. My husband was home to meet with the heating and air workers, as we'd been without air conditioning for several weeks. He turned on the radio and soon an old favorite came one – *Rodeo* by Garth Brooks – which took me back to the days when I was a young girl living in a lovely small Texas town dating a bull rider. While the similarities stop there, the memories did spark a story that has now finally made it into a book.

I am also very grateful to my wonderful critique partners and reviewers over the years. Thanks to Lori, Phyllis, and Lynn who painstakingly went through the original story chapter by chapter and to Jennifer S. who critiqued the entire manuscript. Huge thanks also go to the busy and sweet young ladies Katelyn and Tiffani. You are such a blessing to me as my last sets of eyes before publication!

Other Books by Tracy Wainwright

Nonfiction

Treasures of Healthy Living
Teacher's Manual

Living Praise: a journal of thanks-living

Children's Books

Counting from Creation
Apple vs. Asparagus

Adult Fiction

Her Whole Self

Find out more about the author and her books at:

www.tracywainwright.com

www.facebook.com/tracywainwrightauthorpage

www.twitter.com/TracyWrites4Him

Want to discover new Christian authors?

Join the

Christian Indie Author Readers Group

On Facebook.

Opportunities for free books and giveaways.

http://www.facebook.com/groups/291215317668431/

www.ingramcontent.com/pod-product-compliance
Lightning Source LLC
Chambersburg PA
CBHW070703280626
47159CB00022B/1807

* 9 7 8 0 9 8 9 9 4 8 5 3 1 *